T0193705

"And the Lord said unto Cain, Why art thou wroth? and why is thy countenance fallen? If thou doest well, shalt thou not be accepted? and if thou doest not well, *SIN* lieth at the door. And unto thee shall be *HIS* desire, and thou shalt rule over him." (Genesis 3:6-7 KJV)

THE LIGHT BEARER

7 Days of Light

AUGUST GRACIE

EDITED BY KAREN RIVERA

BALBOA.PRESS

A DIVISION OF HAY HOUSE

Balboa Press books may be ordered through booksellers or by contacting:

Balboa Press
A Division of Hay House
1663 Liberty Drive
Bloomington, IN 47403
www.balboapress.com
844-682-1282

Because of the dynamic nature of the Internet, any web addresses or links contained in this book may have changed since publication and may no longer be valid. The views expressed in this work are solely those of the author and do not necessarily reflect the views of the publisher, and the publisher hereby disclaims any responsibility for them.

The author of this book does not dispense medical advice or prescribe the use of any technique as a form of treatment for physical, emotional, or medical problems without the advice of a physician, either directly or indirectly. The intent of the author is only to offer information of a general nature to help you in your quest for emotional and spiritual well-being. In the event you use any of the information in this book for yourself, which is your constitutional right, the author and the publisher assume no responsibility for your actions.

Any people depicted in stock imagery provided by Getty Images are models, and such images are being used for illustrative purposes only. Certain stock imagery © Getty Images.

Scripture quotations are from the Holy Bible, King James Version (Authorized Version). First published in 1611. Quoted from the KJV Classic Reference Bible, Copyright © 1983 by The Zondervan Corporation.

Print information available on the last page.

ISBN: 979-8-7652-2635-3 (sc)
ISBN: 979-8-7652-2636-0 (e)

Balboa Press rev. date: 05/09/2022

7 DAYS OF LIGHT
The Alert No One Heard

Agent O: Sir, do you feel comfortable enough to tell me the whole story?

It was just a regular night in New York City, a little rain, but Times Square was buzzing just as it has been for over 400 years. The same loud, yet amazing atmosphere it has evolved into still held her blinding brightness, flashing lights, flamboyant characters, tons of cars, and of course extravagant art and theatre. There were millions of people from all over the World in this melting pot of people, nations, tongues and accents, and everything went on as usual in Times Square, even as this strange broadcast went over the air waves of national radio stations, social media outlets, podcasts, and television broadcasts. Yet this report went unnoticed because the World was already used to every kind of emergency and catastrophic event you can think of.

Every conspiracy of every kind was being revealed and created as a new one was solved. The years of misinformation from racist media outlets, satire news, people creating algorithms which create algorithms, life imitating art, the combination of reality and theatrics, where man's every imagination is met, mass shootings and murders go unnoticed and entertainment is easily confused with politics, it has become a time when evil is greatly rewarded and good acts are condemned. At any moment spontaneous wild parties can burst out because it's the shock entertainment era, a good time and yet a dangerous time. People have been literally shot on camera, and the audience loves the gore of this entertainment. These events have become the glitter of the moments in this city, and in the World abroad. The majority of the people walk around like zombies glued to their devices or spend time programming and customizing other electronic mechanisms to make their lives more convenient. All of the thousands of satellite stations which broadcast the World's radio and television aired this strange event. Yet no one really cared to know what was truly happening

Agent O: What was this strange event that no one cared to pay attention to?

Television and radio stations were buzzing with the reports of the strange surges of energy that struck from coast to coast, city to city. Yet, no one payed any attention to this particular brief and sudden event. The news world and its reports were so involved with the event that suddenly struck the Earth for a brief moment, *yet* nothing seemed to happen, *no* real catastrophe. The high-energy surges pounded the entire Earth and even destroyed the Aurora Borealis, but still no one was bothered by this *one* event. Dolphins began changing their swimming patterns, the oceans began to quake at the deepest and darkest parts of all unknown areas of the great blue waters, and all seven continents began to float towards each other, even if at the slightest pace, yet no one cared as people were so heavily invested in their handheld devices, or saving their last dimes to take a trip to Mars to the Disney Space Park and Resort with its tonnage of amenities and a plethora of robots, sites, and features. Also, many new and innovative drones of all sizes flew across the skies delivering packages, foods, and now even mail. VR goggles, automated transportation systems, and automation of Artificial Intelligence had replaced a lot of jobs, but there were still a lot of factory and warehousing jobs people worked because of the complications with robot stress in the warehouses and docks.

The strange thunder and lightning displays occurred across the entire Earth, but it went mostly unnoticed as people were more interested in being entertained instead of informed. After so many centuries of people always living in fear of the End of the World from false information, no one really cared about the next big threat from space, because mankind had become voluntarily unaware of its World and of itself. Political issues and power conflicts, that had always been between larger countries, had also become commonplace between small lands and townships in certain regions. World peace seemed to be on the way via an unlikely man of power in the World who has been sewing the World leaders together as one with his idea of a one-World policy, sweeping them off their feet at an alarming rate with his smooth and powerful words. His big idea of a new monetary system for the entire World seemed to be the key to his campaign of peace.

Agent O: So what else happened? How did we get to this moment?

Inside the headquarters of the Center for E.A.R.T.H. (Extraterrestrial Activities Round The Horizon), the alert warning sounded of extremely dangerous, high-risk extraterrestrial activity in the empty space surrounding the planet. Each unit located around the globe communicates with the headquarters unit located in Los Angeles, California, to ascertain the problem, asking if it's just a drill or the real thing, a serious imminent threat. General R. Vanderpool, who is the head of this top-secret operation, sent out a response after receiving messages from all the other leaders in the secret locations around the globe. "All units—this is not a test, this is HIGH ALERT status code Magma! Be prepared to engage and intercept at any moment at any point over the entire Earth!"

There was blackness and silence, then sudden thundering and lightning. From a quick zoom-in to Earth from outer space down to New York, an individual was suddenly running and frantically looking up above them. In the same instant they ran, they stopped running as if nothing was wrong, but a few yards up from them another person begins running frantically. Then the same thing happens in New Orleans, then Houston, up to Chicago, all over from Detroit down to St. Louis, from Kansas City across to Denver, to Las Vegas, Sacramento, and Los Angeles. There was a man that broke out running erratically in LA, screaming and looking up at the sky, and other pedestrians who see him look up and see nothing; same thing happens where he suddenly stops running and begins walking like nothing ever happened, while a few yards up the block another person begins running in a frenzy.

And as these individual people panic and run, then continue at the pace they were originally walking, a man who seems to be homeless prepares himself to commit suicide by jumping in front of a garbage truck coming toward him at high speed. Yards behind him a man is running in a berserk manner towards him, and in the next second the man began walking normally, the homeless man completes his jump into the speeding garbage truck head-first. The man is knocked unconscious and the garbage truck suffers tremendous damage to its front end. An ambulance is called and the man is transported to the hospital. After being examined by the head trauma unit, everyone is baffled as to why the truck had a dent, and how he was able to survive the impact of such a heavy truck.

They bring the man to an interview area to check the function of his brain, where they discover from his MRI and CAT scan that his entire brain was functioning normally and there was not a trace of head trauma or any immediate results of brain damage due to the blow suffered by the garbage truck. Before the news report about the man could be released, or even one line could be written about this accident, four men dressed in black came into the hospital and swiftly escorted him out on a stretcher. A couple of big guys easily grabbed the limp body off of the stretcher as a rag doll, and hopped into, then departed in an extremely detailed and shiny black van. The van drove away to the outskirts of the city, then disappeared from sight into a hidden tunnel. Reports popped up all over about the incident, and conspiracy theorists have presented it as true in certain groups, and among followers who watch for phenomenal events. There are also reports that some energy source wiped out the Aurora Borealis and readings are off the scale, and supposedly something in the range of 100 nuclear bombs going off at one time.

That is what the report said in detail. Somehow, I can remember it all...

Agent O: Tell me all that you can remember.

…And God called the light Day, and the darkness he called Night. And the evening and the morning were the <u>First Day</u>.

The examining agent was a tall and slender man, and he slightly ducked as he entered the room where the victim of the accident sat quietly. He was a confident yet humble kind of person, an educated man who looked like someone who has mastered plenty of college-level books and a few religious ones in his lifetime.

He neared the area where the subject sat patiently to be examined, then reached into his inner suit-pocket to pull out a pair of designer glasses and began fumbling through his miniature notebook, readying his micro recorder to find out what happened. Glancing down at his calendar, then peering down at his watch to see the minute hand as it ticked, waiting for the perfect moment before he began his interrogation, the subject sitting in front of him broke the ice with a simple question.

What is today?

Sunday, it is now Sunday morning.

Sunday was the time I used to get up early, a little extra earlier than usual because that was the day I would fix breakfast for my family. I would feed them because all week I labored for them. I stood in front of that stove each Sunday and I fixed and served my family breakfast in bed. My wife and all the children would get a treat each and every first day of the week, all three boys and my beautiful wife. It was the beginning of the week and I figured it was made to get a good kick-start for their week. I was raised in the Southern Baptist Church and I went to church all my life, and I did what Mamma said. I would fix that breakfast for my family the first day of the week. I made good ol' grits, eggs, sausage, and fried taters, all accompanied by a tall glass of orange juice. After breakfast, everyone dressed and we went to church. I did this for years.

This was a normal thing for you? Something you did regularly as a routine thing? Was it something that truly pleased you?

Oh yes, I was very pleased to serve my maker and my family on Sundays. It was my biggest joy.

The two men sat silently with each other for some moments and then the man began to laugh. It seemed a bit unusual, but the Examiner was used to all kinds of cases of tragedy and how people cope with the circumstances. The laugh turned into a hysterical laugh, one that would seem inappropriate to many, but the laughter then mellowed out to a slight chuckle, then into a mere shaking of his head.

Sir, you ok? Is anything bothering you at this moment?

No, no, no, I am fine. I am fine sir, but that was not me laughing at all.

The agent gave the man a suspicious side-eye and look of amazement because it was clearly obvious who was laughing. He knew that the man who sat adjacent from him burst into laughter most likely due to the loss of his family from tragedy. He has seen many cases like this and inwardly he sympathized with the patient.

I did not just hear you laugh—is what you're telling me?

I, I know I didn't laugh. That was not me.

Who was it?

I do not know, sir.

Well, apparently, I don't know either. I guess in time we'll just have to find out.

Yes, I hope we will, because that was very unusual. It was not me.

I would like to meet this person one day. Do you think you can arrange this for me?

Sir, I tell you it wasn't me who laughed, and I don't know how to arrange this meeting that you want.

The men stared in each other's direction, somehow never actually making eye contact. It was an awkward time for both of them. They sat there speechless and sized each other up, but not in an aggressive manner, just sort of gauging and establishing trust between each other. The big decision to trust or not to trust pulsated through the twenty-by-twenty-foot room. The subject lay on a couch comfortably, and the Examiner sat in a padded chair with his legs crossed. The agent scribbled some words on his electronic notepad as his micro-recorder captured everything.

Can you tell me what happened at the scene of the accident you were in? Exactly what happened back there and what was going through your head when it occurred?

Well, I really don't know what happened. I was tired and I was at the end of my emotional string. I mean, I was ready to die and it seems like God won't let me kill myself.

So, God would not let you kill yourself?

I am sitting right here to tell you. I literally planned it out perfectly, to destroy myself in the quickest way I could. I stood on the edge of the road and waited for the right moment for the truck to get close enough to not notice me. I did not want the driver to hit his brakes or slow down. That would have hindered my plan to get this life over with. But something happened to me that I cannot explain. Something hit me in my back, and as I think about it, I truly don't know what happened to me. I know I was dead, I know it was over, and soon I'd be able to see my family again. I'd wake up in Heaven above and be able to see my Creator and all those who died in the way of Christ. But I ain't dead and this ain't Heaven above.

Out of thin air, there was that mysterious laughter again. It was louder and the Examiner raised his eyebrow at the man.

I know, it was not you. But you can continue, sir.

I know I was dead, but something protected me from what I was about to do to myself.

What happened to your family, if you don't mind discussing this obviously tragic event? Sometimes it's good to get these things out of our minds and speak out loud to someone the very things that haunt us.

Honestly, I have never spoken about this, and since I'm still here, I guess it won't hurt anything.

The subject repositioned himself on the couch and got more comfortable, sighed deeply, then began his story.

It happened a few years ago. I was a preacher at a small community church in rural Oklahoma. I was the good kid. I always tried to be the best person, so I went back home to preach the good news because there was no one else who wanted to pick up the torch in my family. I come from a family of preachers of the good word. I didn't know him, but my Grandfather, my uncles and quite a few of my older cousins before me were all pastors. Ed, Lester, and Tobias, now those boys were some good preachers and always told the truth on that good news!

The mysterious chuckle returned even louder, and they both looked at each other a bit concerned because clearly both of them heard the strange laughter of another person in the room with them.

I know that was not you. Now who is it? I don't know who can answer that question for us.

The subject moved the IV lines in his arm to the side as he poured water into his glass from a pitcher on the small table next to the couch he sat on, and quickly gulped the liquid down to the last drop. The men briefly looked at each other, then continue their conversation. The man again repositioned himself on the couch and gently interlocked his hands across his lower chest, got as comfortable as he could, and continued the story.

When Tobias was getting too old to preach, well there was no one else to do the job. All of my other cousins and even Tobias's sons were all too corrupt to continue the family ministry. Heck I even remember a vague rumor that everyone was afraid to take up the position because we were some kind of way kin to ol' John Brown of Missouri. I wasn't ever afraid of anything, so they reached in the hat and approached me. I thought about it and then after a little time, I accepted the responsibility that comes with being in charge of those sheep looking for God. I was already married to my wife Jean for ten years and we had two children. Every Monday morning when I was up to get ready for work, Jean would have my coffee ready for me. Always thinking of others before self, that is just how she was. My two children were nine and four, two boys. They said they wanted to be a preacher just like me. Can you believe that? Like me. That is why I loved them more than anything. My sons, Onan and Eric, I miss them all so much. But every Monday and all the week I was up working. Like the good book says, a man who does not work does not eat. I did just like it said, I worked, and then I preached every Sunday. I had saved up a lot of cash from working because I even worked on Saturdays. Our goals were simple, just for me to save as much money as possible to retire and then preach full-time, and then pass it all down to the boys. Everything was perfect, our life together was so prosperous, and we loved everyone just like Jesus said. I know I have done all the things I was taught, and did my very best to always walk as a man of God.

The man took a deep breath and ground his teeth just slightly. He shook his head in despair and sadness because he knew the words he would say may not be but an inch from blasphemy. So many things and so many unanswered questions swirled in his head. Full of sadness and pride, he regrettably spoke the words he thought he would never utter to another human being.

I feel I hate God! All the years of my life I longed to know God and after pledging my life to him, doing all of these great works in the name of Jesus, all of it was for absolutely nothing! There was no protection for my wife and children, and they were taken away from me when we were just getting started with our lives! We were the example of what a good Christian family is and how a family should be! We got up every day and praised the Lord Jesus and we prayed every day as a family! We served the community, we always volunteered and helped everyone in our community! I preached that gospel the best ever in that town, and I brought a lot of people out of the bounds of that evil alcohol, smoking cigarettes, and illegal drugs! I helped almost the entire community convert to Jesus and I did a lot of fundraisers for our community! I did a whole damn lot of work for Jesus and he rewards me by killing my family in a car accident! What kind of God am I worshipping if he allows my family—his servant's family—to die!? But the alcoholic driving almost a hundred miles an hour without a seatbelt, mind you, slams headfirst and directly into my family who is traveling the opposite direction, killing them all! I watched them buckle their seat belts before they left the house and I even waved good-bye to them as they pulled off! The guy flew through his windshield and he lived!

The laughter suddenly filled the room, and both the man and agent were startled and looked at each other. The agent was a cool-headed kind of guy who simply sat there without breaking a sweat. The man filled with schizophrenia from years of wandering the highways of the USA filled with rushing anger and began to yell out to the laughter which filled the room and faded. He sat up and looked around in all directions, making brief eye contact with the agent, yelling:

Wait, are you laughing at me?!

No, we were both looking at each other, sir.

What is going on in my head!

The laughter returned and the man sat upright and began to chuckle and bursts out into laughter again.

He said his wife and sons were killed in an accident. Yes, indeed they died in 2010. He has been wandering around aimlessly for fifteen years. Here it is 2025 and he is still mourning for flesh bags he cannot redeem from the dirt? Adamites are yet and still ignorant.

I thought you were not laughing?

I guess it depends on which you, that you are speaking to.

Picking up his recorder, the agent spoke into the device and made some more notes.

Which you, are you now, sir? I have only met one you so far.

I am not a part of him at all. I am my own self. This guy is just another weakling and deserves to die like all of you Adamites. I can now assume that this is the work of Old Mike.

Sir, I know you have lost a lot, and that great loss has caused you to develop another personality to compensate for the stress of your loss. I have dealt with many of these kinds of cases. I can help you.

The problem with you filthy Adamites is you think you can help or resolve any problem or issue any being has, yet you still treat each other worse than rabid animals. You kill each other, battle each other over lands and possessions, and in the same breath you are giving me a false hope of you helping me? You cannot help resolve my issue, not even a little bit.

Sir, if I may, you tried to commit suicide. You just expressed to me your hatred for God and now your disdain for these *Adamites* you speak about? I am only trying to collect valuable information to help you with your situation. How did we end up in the realm of the evils of humanity? Can you tell me more about this anger that you have towards humanity?

The main ingredient is the fact that death connects all humans, and all of mankind doesn't realize they are the same species. Simple facts which men and women seem to always miss. There is an order to everything.

Sir, what of the story of the woman Eve being the mother of all humans born, she being the first woman?

The Adam came before Eve. The Adam named all animals and was living life to the fullest, eating from The Garden and learning from the Prince of Kings. He existed decades before the Eve, which came after him. She had to catch up to the same level of knowledge that Adam possessed for decades before she was created. This is why women mature before men. The gap of time and the space of learning that had to be compensated for, in order for her to catch up to her spouse's wisdom, is truly amazing; the Eve was so phenomenal. This simple fact is known from culture to culture and people to people across the entire Earth, that the Eve was the helpmeet prepared for the Adam and had superior thinking capacity to resolve problems to make life even better for the Adam.

So, the man came before the woman is what you're telling me? I don't believe some things, not all things, but this is something in which I truly don't believe.

The Eve had to be taken from the Adam for numerous reasons. The King of Heavens, in the total complexity of his own simple thoughts, has every bit of his reasons on why he decided to make the Eve come out of the Adam. But to just give you a hint on why, the True Creator of all things does amazing things in the sight of men. His thoughts and ways are not shallow, but can be comprehended by those who seek his foreknowledge and understanding of all of the things he creates, and the reasons and patterns of all things. Only a few will he give the glory to complete the purpose of the Adamites, to be the first of their kind to be inducted and adopted into The_Royal Family of the King of Heavens and his Prince The Word.

Sir, that just doesn't make sense to me. Someone taking a bone from a man's body and creating another person with it?

The male and the female are one, the same species. It is kind of how you say: the yin and the yang, the peanut butter and jelly, of all things made whole. Two separate systems, yet the same system. The first of its kind ever created. Destined to be the ones to inherit the Kingdom that will be on the Earth. The same Earth they were made from.

Ok, so how do these two systems work?

The Adam and its Eve were designed to reproduce together in a psychological, physical, compassionate entanglement that you now call "lovemaking."

Any red-blooded man or woman on Earth understands what lovemaking is. Please, wow me.

My brethren, the Legion and I, literally burst into laughter at the hypocrisy of you all. They are nonetheless just acts of putrid lust. The way you Adamites perform in these vile physical forms of pleasure are lower than that which even the animals do. Just disgusting lust and smooth words to sugar-coat the acts which anger and embarrass the King of Heavens, these things that are done outside of the marriages you all conjoin in, and to have the absolute nerve to label it as "hooking up" or other expletives which it is called. The sacred act of conjoining as one has been tossed out the window with the vulgarities and obscenities over the centuries, since the existence of the species of the Adamites.

Wow. Are there any other concerns or disagreements you have with this species, the Adamites?

The same species with its many varieties has henceforth moved forward to kill itself continually ever since the first-born of the prototype Adam and its Eve. The offspring of the Adam was to do just as its predecessor before it.

Adam was a prototype? A prototype for what?

It was to be given a half, and then again over and over it was to multiply, and it was to teach the ordinances of the King of Heavens. And in the given time in those ages, the Adamites would be granted access to be completely changed, the final metamorphosis into what it was created to be.

In detail, can you tell me what is this Adamite to become in this metamorphosis?

If you insist.

The daughters of the Adam were given to each son in the beginning, for the building of the Earth's populace of people. Some cultures of humans will see this methodology as offense or even as incest. Yet this creation does not even realize what was happening, or what was going on at the time of the first thought conceived by The King of Heavens, to move forward with creating this type of being. It should be remembered or known, that the King of Heavens is a being that was never created or made; he is very complex in his thoughts and yet very simple in his ways. He is very sensitive at the thought that this creation does not even consider him or his power. This is why The Word is the only one who deals with the workings and beings of the Earth, The Word is His Ambassador, and His Overseer of all the creations that deal with the carnal and invisible of this entire planet, the systems of stars and uninhabited planets, which stretches farther than man's greatest imaginations. There are many faults of the Adamites. The blatant disrespect of each other for no reason, some humans are even more evil than the Fallen Legion. Some are so wicked they even consider the means of working hand-in-hand with the Fallen Legion to receive the precious stones in the Earth that are used for mediums of exchange. The fear of God is now turned to the Fallen Legion by means of blood lust. But there is a difference between Adamites in these last centuries just as it was in the days before Noah's Deluge, which you now call "Gilgamesh's epic."

Very interesting. I am familiar with Gilgamesh, and different theories surrounding the subject.

It was 2:00 p.m. and the time seemed to just stop. Yet the man continued his long and dragging story. The funny part is, the story became very interesting due to the history he was able to recall of over five-thousand years of human histories. The man continued his calm cadence of perfectly patterned thoughts and he wound back the hands of time from the year 2025 to the first years of humankind.

What is different from this group of Adamites, as you say, from the group before the Great Deluge?

The last millennia of Adamites were different because The King of Heavens decided they were not going to destroy all humans and begin all over again with a new Adam. Neither will they create a whole new flock of humans to do their will by force. They prefer free-will participants and they have blessed humankind and the other celestial creations with this freedom, the same thing the disobedient Adamites destroyed, which is your very own free will. That same free will should be reinforced with discipline and obedience, along with self-control, to reach the goal that the King has for all humanity. The King of Heavens is very detailed and very tactical at all things he does. This is no experiment by far, this is the very first and just may be the very last creation of humankind. The King of Heavens simply left the task up to The Word, who took the one called Nuwah and made him into the town crier, the servant to the people on this side of the Creation.

What does this "side of Adam's Creation" mean? I'm not understanding.

The same DNA which was in Adam is in the Noah, which is a grandson of the Adam. The Noah is simply a latter version of the Adam, better and stronger in faith and stature, tall and beautiful just like his grandfather the Adam. The Noah responded just as The Word knew it would, when given the same scenarios as the other lower-grade Adamites which had populated in great numbers across the region of Eden. The first generations all were tall as trees and almost as strong as the original Adam. Most of them understood the sin of Cain and it seemed as though things could change, yet when they intermingled with the daughters of Cain in the early years, they were easily persuaded to do evil. But as time went by these creations seemed to do even more horrible things by themselves without any influence. Even at the time of Lamech, not the father of Noah but a relative of his, who was disinherited years before the Noah was ever born. The name Lamech was used for Noah's father in hopes of redeeming the glory lost by this evil Lamech's actions of murder. The Adamites were all different shades of deep black and brown, even down to tan and paler hues of these tones. Each one had the same DNA as the first Adam the prototype. The distribution of DNA was not made to be equal; the DNA was designed to change and even contrast according to how the body was nurtured and fed and depending on whosoever the parents of the offspring were. If the body was nurtured with unclean foods, it was not resilient to diseases because what foods that are put into the body determine the overall health of the body. The Adamite has a body that is perfectly designed and it is also nurtured with words one speaks. Yes, the bodies of the Adamite can self-heal, something known for centuries; in fact, it is designed to live forever if the right commands are obeyed by this soul. But this age of Adamites, too, did not take well to understanding and holding onto good things to teach and live, and pass down to the generations to come afterwards. They began to oppress and murder and steal, well the main things that lead to all kinds of evil acts. What is way worse than this, they even began to eat each other, not often, but on occasion there are still to this day different types of human blood drinking and abductions amongst the tribes of the Earth, which are all related in every sense, and now it is translated into what is called kidnapping and sex trafficking, or the ways of Moloch—a system I created. It must have been a period of observation for The Word, he is very highly intelligent and sometimes he takes his time before deciding to destroy you or to give you mercy, but you will most definitely pay for your transgressions in some form or fashion. He does have compassion, but not as much as the King of Heaven. The King has the biggest heart of all, so he left it up to The Word to come up with a solution for what to do with these now murderous and disobedient Adamites. Things went bad after the death of the Adam, who kept all in line and in order after he showed complete repentance and decided to continue to follow the things The Word was teaching him, even after his exile out of the Garden of Eternity in Eden, Persian Gulf. The first Adam quickly realized what The Word was trying to teach him all those years, about Eternity and what it was and how to obtain it, but he was not able to. So once the Adam learned all that was needed after the death of his second son, Abel, he passed all of this knowledge to a new seed that would carry the ordinances of the King of Heaven on to the generations of Adam. Through the new seed of Seth is the way The Word taught Adam how to redeem his children from the destruction he knew would befall the majority of his children and grandchildren. Because The Word gave Adam the Prophecy of the future and it was passed through all of the first-born sons of the one called Seth on down to Noah, the same DNA and knowledge was passed on through to Noah who was chosen to champion the generations of the Adam on to a new time, facing the new challenges of humankind. Oddly, the funny part is that Noah and his sons were literally the shortest people of their time, though they were very tall. Noah himself stood about 7'7", with his sons and even their wives all standing in variation between 6'9" and 10' tall. The sons of Noah are the three_tribes, which populated this entire plane with the billions of humans seen in all shapes, sizes, colors, and traditions. I have always been in awe that Adamites have never looked back at these facts of the matter, but have always tried to separate themselves from their true power as being together as one. Even in your science it teaches that the atom is the building block of the Universe, but what kind of power does one have, only knowing this? What is the power that knowing the very body you dwell in is made up of atoms, which are bonded together to form one solid soul? The one single entity, the soul, which is the body, is the sum total of each and every human that lives and dies in this World.

How does this DNA help me to live forever, since you are in the telling mode, sir?

I want you to imagine if you could create those very atoms. You, being the builder of those very atoms and having endless possibilities? The power of knowing how to create those very atoms from thin air and creating the invisible can be done, but not in the infantile stage of the Adamite. The Adamite does not realize that it cannot live forever unless it becomes one body under the order of the King of Heavens. There is no understanding in the Adamite to even realize its full potential and reason for being created. The Adamite, along with its actions, is ok with being a third-class creation that rots and decays more each day after its birth. The aging process is simply a ripening stage in which the soul gets older just as fruit in a bowl on someone's counter or refrigerator. Each day it lives it decays, and what does it do with the life it is given? It indulges in Sin; my spirit dwells in them who follow Sin. Through the followers of the order of Nimrod ben Kush the Kushian, King of Babylonia, fallen Son of God, who chose me to lead him to eternal fame through the generations of mankind.

But sir, you are sitting here with me.

Yes, we are in the future. Here we are today and the same ancient story is still alive. The Adamites hold on to the prosperity of Nimrod and his traditions through many religions, which are the exact same as the occult practices of the pagan gods from his time of old, and now, new days.

Ok, so how did you do it? How did you make the World plunge into darkness, sir?

I have strategically directed the Adam away from uniting to become one under the banner of the King of Heavens, to become the divided religious freaks and psychos you see today, you are very welcome. This is why the unity of the Adam will fail; this is why lots of the Adamites will join the Fallen in the second death of eternity. The way to become the new Adam is to follow the instructions of the King of Heavens above. This simplicity is the only way to live forever and ever in peace. There is absolutely no other way that is humanly possible to accomplish this final stage of Adam, to avoid the second eternal death.

So this King just wants all of mankind to simply submit to him?

Yes, the same Adamites were broken off into different languages and lands. They now have the audacity to say they are not the same people. The Word decided to downsize the height, size, and strength of the human. He even gave them different facial features to bring more of a variety to the world of people. He lessened their strength to stop takeovers by juggernauts who possessed great strength, and prima donnas who possessed great beauty. The Adamites of Noah's grace have more power given to them by the power of words, not just in great physical strength.

Ok, the Tower of Babel and its surrounding area is where Nimrod ruled, but what of the Nephilim? Since you are close to the topic of giants, enlighten me?

The majority of the tallest Adamites were literally killed off in battles waged centuries ago. These were nicknamed Nephilim, which is merely another word for giant or Neanderthal. But even the biggest humans have the same DNA as the ones who are shorter than they. Even through all of these generations of the Adamites' existence they cannot seem to grasp two single facts that link the entire species together, due to pure ignorance created by propaganda and deceit. They cannot see that any man on the face of this planet can impregnate any fertile woman on this entire Earth, and the fact that all of mankind dies.

The mystery of procreation, and the promise of death, are two small facts that link mankind one to another. And it is very simple, but of course, mankind has made these things irrelevant. Mankind has taken itself away from the purpose in which it was created by evils and lusts of their own imaginations of self, and self-worship. Even the simplicity of seeing the facts of this matter, and the proof in the animal kingdom which clearly shows you that no other animals outside of its own species can reproduce without that of its own species. This is why the Adamites cannot move forward and the reason the Legion can continue to succeed and to influence many to follow them to the second death of eternity.

The agent swiftly writes down some notes.

What is this "second death of eternity" that you have mentioned?

The man does not answer the question asked, but instead continues talking on the subjects he felt were most important.

The Adamite does not see this simple logic, yet will continue to want to have rulership over each other in the most horrible ways. It will kill its own father, mother, brother, sister—anyone it sees as interfering with the evil it has plotted to do. The evil it plots is always of its own will, but it is quick to blame my Legion's doings. I truly find that appalling in every sense, the intelligence Adamites wish to award themselves to have. They have divided themselves, made themselves seem as though they are different, when they all have the same type of blood. Though there are four types of blood—Shem, Ham and Japheth, and the blood of the Adam through Seth, which was in Noah—this blood type was passed to Noah by mere simplicity. This understanding solidified the covenant between Noah and the King of Heavens through his Minister and Prince, The Word. Each first-born son from Seth to Noah believed the instructions and future happenings which were beyond their years. Even the one named Enoch—this Adamite is the example of what the purpose of mankind is. He is the example that Adam should have been in even a lesser amount of time, and this same blood that ran through Enoch also ran through the first-born sons of Seth. This same blood ran through the veins of Adam, created by The Word, passed to Noah, and then on to the three sons of the covenant, Shem, Ham, and Japheth, in which the entire world of Adamites gets their different shades of "black" from. They range from the darkest color of the captivatingly beautiful onyx stone to the deep white of the most beautiful snow. Do not be alarmed or surprised or offended, this is the simplicity of the divine, the facts of matter, which the hierarchies of Adamites in all of their subgroups in this last age have denied. Each subculture of Adamites have tried to make the Adam to physically look as each of your groups look through literature and imagery. Adam was perfect; if you took each and every human born in the Age of Noah and combined them all, they could not even equal a drop of what the Adam was, or should I say is? Most humans are just small shavings off of a big tree; mere peons compared to its original, the Adam. I still stand in awe at the ignorance of the Adamites of Noah's age. It truly amazes me. All of them are the same, yet they battle each other for the same power and abilities they all can obtain together as one. Yet they still fight for power over the nations and each other.

The agent leans over a bit towards the end table near the couch he sat on, grabs his cup of water and takes a big sip. He then scribbles a little more information onto his notepad.

So what would you say is mankind's biggest problem?

Well, simply put—by one man, Sin entered the World.

Man thinks that Sin entered the World by the way of a man and woman eating an apple in the Garden of Eden. I have always marveled at these flesh-and-blood creatures' ability to turn the simplest things into the most fabricated fairy tales they can imagine. Sin began long before man ever existed. In fact, I created the very sin that you participate in each and every day of your lives. Sin is my creation, the only thing I was able to create. I tried to cooperate, I tried to deny and fight the creation of these ignorant beings to the Board of the Legions, and even after expressing the concerns of my Legion to the board, our voices were not enough to ever go against the King of Heavens. Sin became my creation, the one thing that a being who was also created, could have created on its own. I had a mission to multiply it across the entire world of man, my very own Adam, the Adam which would kill the Adam of the King of Heavens. How dare he not acknowledge us as his only sons? We are the ones who kept the order for him, and he simply forgot about us? This is why I created Sin. Sin entered the Kingdom of Heaven by one angel, by one son. Lucifer was the bearer of light; Prince to the King of Heaven, and King of the Legion of Cherubs of Light and Honor. The first-born of Cherubim angels, the beauty of all things created was embedded in him, the power of the air and its waves in my wings, the sounds of the air in my palms, the most preciously formed by the hands of the Prince of the King. I was the one who stood for the King; I was willing to make him understand that this carnal creation should not have been created! So I created the thing that is killing his creation to this very day; my first-born, who I named Sin. How did I create Sin? Sin was simply the reverse of the order of the things set forward by the King of Heavens. My Legions' rebellion resulted in a war that lasted for thousands of years only because the King of Heavens was deciding what to do with our Legion of powerful cherubs, which cannot die, as all Celestials do not expire. Sin was with us and my child grew and the more he grew, the more powerful he became through mimicking the ways of The Word of God; the One True Prince of the King. I became a god, and Sin, my Prince, we both dwelled in the celestial realm above in the Kingdom of Heavens. My Prince and I were able to capture one-third of believers in the Kingdom of Heaven, and once the King of Heavens decided what to do with the one-third, he called forth the third-born angel, Mikhail the Prince of the Legion of the Princes of War and Peace, the Most Powerful warriors ever created, embedded with full allegiance to the King of Heavens and his Prince The Word. They were the ones who tossed us down to this vile Earth to await our judgment; and while we do so, we have walked up and down and all through this Earth in its darkest abysses, and the places man will never see. We have been in all corners of this Earth and have seen all there is to see in the Earth. We did not know what he was doing—we did not know what he was doing! But there was no turning back after creating Sin, and as we wait, Sin has become more powerful nowadays in the realm of man. There was a moment in time, a long time ago in pure darkness of this World, when The Word appeared. We thought judgment was upon us at that moment because he is not a cuddly ruler. He is precise, perfect, patient, and pursuant of only following the will of the order set forth by the King of Heaven with full unbreakable obedience to the King. We prepared for punishment, yet he gave us mercy, if you would call it that. But I would say he gave us time that ticked down to our very expiration of existence. Each and every one of us was marked for death; at that very moment The Word stopped speaking to us, and then you truly become desolate beings. He soon then began the work to create the environments for the Adam. He worked for seven long days non-stop without any rest or breaks from his work. This was the plan that was put forth on the table of the King of Heaven and it would only have taken a literal seven days for Adam to flourish and become eternal, to become a Celestial, and also be a judge of us? This carnal being? How dare he judge the Legion of Light and Honor? How could this be? The Word showed everyone the plan from the end to the beginning.

The Beginning, From the End

He had already formed the Earth and created the environments for man in the five days needed, animals and all plant life, from the air humans breathe to the sun, moon and stars, even other planets to gaze at. He made everything needed to have a safe environment to support carnal forms. From the very end of this flesh form we were seeing the multitude of new Gods. The King of Heavens effortlessly figured out how to create more Gods that looked physically just as he and his Prince's celestial form. The Word said, "This will be a brand-new hierarchy of eternity, the first of its kind, standing for truth and light, and everlasting reverence for the King." We were so ignorant not to understand the bigger picture until it was revealed ages afterwards. We did not have the patience needed to exist in the Kingdom of Heaven. We only saw these new Princes as rulers over us, this disgusting vile organism formed from this ooze-filled Earth that we Devils have walked in and out, and up and down, and now we have to bow to this evil abomination?! This place is only blessed to still exist because the King of Heavens himself wants to live down here and set his kingdom on this planet, for some strange reason.

Very interesting? So what is this Kingdom of Heaven above like?

The Kingdom above is so beautiful, if you could only see it. My last time seeing the Kingdom was when I challenged the King of Heavens for his beloved Job. All of the Legions were called to the great hall to hearken to the King of Heavens and his Word speak on a matter concerning the Adamites. I alone was called to enter the great hall of the Kingdom of Heaven and I stared at the thousands or perhaps millions of empty seats located behind the throne of the King. The fact of just knowing these were reserved for the Adamites who will become eternal to rule over all angels and things, it burned me with jealousy. The Word spoke on the behalf of the King and one of the Adamites named Job was mentioned. This Adamite is one of the blessed of the King of Heavens and I became infuriated with hatred to my core, and I blurted out at the fact he called this flesh-being PERFECT. Nothing is perfect except me, the first-born of all ministering Celestials, embedded with all things precious! I challenged The Word for the life of Job so that we could return to Heaven. I blurted out in ignorance, "If Job is perfect, then perfect does not rebel against the King. If Job the perfect rebels, then The Word is wrong and the banishment of the Legion of the Truth and Light is a wrong judgment, for I was made Perfect also."

(1Ezekiel 28)

The interviewer jots down more notes in a flurry as he was intrigued by this story he's never heard before, for the mythological cadence seemed to be reality, but at the same instant, caused him to be caught between two worlds. One world made sense, yet the other world was traditional to him.

What happened when you blurted out those arrogant words to The Word?

The Word, as he is so good at doing, called my bluff and allowed me to test him to the fullest, but I was commanded not to kill him no matter what. If I was successful, the Legion could be reinstated into their place in the Kingdom of Heaven. The King and his Word literally know everything, absolutely everything, and this is a matter of fact. We creations keep forgetting this fact for some odd reason. We forget this so quickly. He knows who his Chosen are and what he will use them for in each generation of all his creations. Remember, the Adamites were created effortlessly in a matter of minutes, but in your time, mere seconds. After all the pain and suffering I caused Job, he never departed from his faith in the King of Heavens and knowledge of what his gift to mankind is, to be just as he is. I could not get him to break! This was the absolute last chance we had to make it home, and it did not work; all that was done to him, he would not speak against the King of Heavens.

He would not die because he had the strength of Noah inside of him sewn in the allegiance to the King of Heavens and his purpose.

(2 Job 2:1-6)

What happened to you and the Legion after you lost terribly against The Word?

After my challenge I was sent away, again, and he has only commanded me from this carnal world full of filth and these disgusting one-headed creatures that do not deserve to wear the appearance of the King of All creations of things seen and invisible. I cannot enter back into the Kingdom of Heaven above ever again, since I tried to shun the King, and his Word, in the presence of the Holy Congregation of All Legions of Angels of Righteousness. Even worse, is the fact that I caused the fall of one-third of an innumerable Legion of Angels; I have harmed too many.

How did you get all of mankind to sin, per se?

I waited patiently in the garden after the creation of the Adam, and I witnessed the creation of the latter part, the Eve. I waited patiently, so patiently, then I whispered Sin into her ear at the right moment. Once I planted the seed of Sin into her ear, I watched it grow and spread like a wildfire through all the generations of Adams. It spread on both sides of the creation from Adam to Noah. It moved forward to the present, to the worst and last generations of the children of Noah. The three prototypes of the latter side of the Great Deluge, even till today as we speak, which is leading up to the Seventh Day, the Revealing of the Kingdom of the Prince.

(3 Revelation 19:11-21)

Do you mind telling me more about your past, and some more about the Adam and Eve, and Sin?

In the beginning, before I understood, I thought it would take brute force to destroy this creation, but the first man Adam; that son of God, was stronger than any of us Cherub angels. This is why I simply watched him for decades. Four long decades I watched him. He was a highly intelligent being, and he learned very quickly.

Was he ever an infant?

No, Adam was a fully-grown man. I watched as The Word commanded and, as he spoke, it all happened through the Hands of God; which are powerful angels, but it sucks to be them as they are just like the hand which scared the life out of Belshazzar the Gentile, son of Nebuchadnezzar. They wrote that hilarious message in the stone walls of his palace. The Hands of God are simply Angels who are shaped like hands, and I watched these brethren of mine as they dug this man out of the Earth. It was the most amazing thing I have ever seen and the most hated thing in my life. For this very act was the very thing I protested in the Kingdom of Heaven.

(4 Daniel 5:1-6, 17, 24-31)

What would be the second most amazing thing you have ever seen in your lifetime?

The second most amazing thing I saw was EVE. This was more than amazing.

The interviewer saved data and exported it, and prepared to write some more notes on his electronic notepad.

How did it happen? Do you recall anything?

Let's see, four decades and Adam was about forty years old, so The Word induced sleep and commanded the Hands of God to move and they went inside of him and literally pulled a rib out of his side. It was painless, the Hands of God are precise in every manner The Word commands them, and remember that mankind is nothing but a molded piece of clay. If they were commanded to deliver pain, he most definitely would have felt every sliver of pain beyond imagination.

I understand, very clever. Can you continue, please?

That rib was taken and the components of that rib were fashioned into a version of feminine skeletal system very similar to that of the Adam. In similar process, the Eve was formed out of the bone of the Adam as she was pulled from him as holding a single mass of clay in your palms, then pulling your hands away from each other, forming two, but both from a single mass of clay that was in your palms to begin. It was simply amazing, and it cannot be repeated by any being, though many have tried and think they are accomplishing definite creation. Adam named her Eve. My goodness he loved her, he loved her so much. It was a love I have never seen any man on Earth after Adam display. It was the very first true love I have ever witnessed. It was the way he looked at her, how he smiled, and he did not touch her for Seven years, they just talked each and every day and did everything together.

(5 Genesis 2:21-25)

Seven years and no relations?

Yes, at the time appointed they conceived Cain, and a year later, Abel. I observed them both, their interactions and conversations, how he taught her and cared for her. There was no violence, only peace, there was no one to fight, no wars, no nations, only them.

If it were only these people, how did you kill them?

What could I possibly use on this entire Earth to kill them because

Adam would have surely stopped me? He was the prototype, the perfect carnal man, the second Son of God, when truly I am the second Son of God. Next to the Prince, it was me, until I was cast out. The one thing I understand is jealousy, with it you destroy man.

Was it difficult to access the Eve, to whisper to her?

I simply just did something she liked, kindness and courtesy. She was even commanded not to utter one word to me, so I literally killed her with kindness. I coined that term long ago. I am still getting paid royalties for that, by the way, and killing people with my form of kindness is

what I do.

Are there any details as to how you "killed her with kindness"?

I love jewels, if you could only see me. She passed near my area and I shouted out to her, "Oh! Beautiful onyx goddess of the Most High God, Wife of the Son of God, Adam born of the Earth! My goddess I am in need of your help, for I have stumbled upon a stone and it is stuck in my hoof. It hurts, and I do need your help, my goddess." This was the moment I preyed on her compassion. I locked eyes with the goddess Eve, and with the saddest kitten eyes I could perform, I made all four of my faces—the lion's head, the face of a man, an eagle's head, and my oxen face—bow as low as I possibly could to the ground and cried my heart out. This was something I thought I would never do, and the irony kills me—wait, that is my saying also. But the good thing for me was that I was able to prey on her compassion and her ignorance of what death was.

I don't think I clearly understand what you mean? Can you explain a little more?

Adam was so in love he did not think about order or the sense of it all, when she spoke to me, and she said, "Poor creature."

So upon the instant she decided to speak to you, she was destroyed?

I got her at that very instant, the moment she opened her mouth to acknowledge me, she was cut off from the inheritance of the Kingdom of Heaven, and she was cut off from the promise. This was the sweetest thought for me, because at that very moment, I bought myself some more time to destroy Adam and all of his generations.

When did she acknowledge you?

It was the sixth year of her being when I approached her. It was the only opportunity I had, and it had to be timed just right! Sometimes I look back to this point in my life and wonder if I ever had a chance to repent? Oh well, it's too late for me, I'm just too prideful to do that.

She was six years old? Wait, sir. You will please have to explain this to me, it sounds very strange.

Time is nothing to him, the King of Heavens is "Father Time," and he is the Father of all things seen and unseen. I bet you knew that. So let me explain to you something important. The very minute she opened her mouth to speak to me, it was the death of mankind. Now all I had to do was keep her engaged in casual conversation and keep her smiling. So I gave her various compliments each day. Just small words, nothing overbearing or too long-winded of a conversation. Then one day I asked her a question that even provoked The Word to intervene. I asked her if she knew that she was naked? My goddess, my beautiful Onyx queen, do you know that you are walking around naked? Not to question your intelligence at all, but to understand your tradition.

(6 Genesis 3:1-3, 7-11)

Can you explain more about this tradition?

Remember she asked me, what is being naked? So I stood tall and spread my wings that wrapped around my entire body and then she could see my covering. She saw all of the Sardis stones: topaz, diamond, beryl, onyx, jasper, sapphire, emerald, carbuncle, and gold. Eve marveled at my precious covering, the same material crap Adamites chase after like a cat for catnip. Yes, she fell for it, but she understood me, and the strange thing is I viewed her as my only friend. At that moment she looked down at her breasts, at her arms, her torso, and lower parts, her sacred place, and then her legs and her feet. She observed me once more, then walked up to me and touched the jewels of my covering, walked completely around me and marveled at my covering, gliding her jet-black hand around me, touching each type of jewel which covered me. She walked directly up to me and looked me in the eyes and said, "How can I have a covering like this? Are not there anymore stones like this? How can I make a covering?" I walked directly up to the nearest tree and grabbed the largest leaves there were and we fashioned the leaves together, and the funny part was she never noticed that at the outermost edge of the garden were the rest of the angels who looked like me, but were not covered like me, because I was more special. Also, at this time the King of Heavens did not mandate the Chains of Darkness upon all Angels above and the Fallen. So it always amazed me that she never noticed them. I became the center of her attention after showing her how to make a skirt and covering with the beautiful and colorful leaves of the great trees of the garden.

(7 Hosea 10:4, 12-13, Ezekiel 28:13-17)

So was this the literal Garden of Eden, the Garden of God Almighty?

Yes, it is the Garden of Eden hidden in the Persian Gulf Region for safekeeping until his return; that's right, you already know. There is no other garden on Earth where The Word dwelled in or visited, it has only been Eden. So I showed her many things and gave her only small suggestions. In just a couple hours per day we spent time together learning new things.

How much time did *you* spend with the Eve?

In the time of Adam, time was literally infinite; there was no forward or backward way of defining time or existence because infinite beings do not need a time factor, but this is what the sun and moon were commissioned to do, keep time. Once again, Adam's creation and children were designed to live forever. So the time and days spent is nothing like you are trying to make sense of in your mind because only Celestials can understand infinity. So, with that being said, I taught her with suggestions, for many days. I was like her girlfriend, her best friend. Everything Adam taught her I was able to help make suggestions to what could be an alternative to what he taught her. I was able to change the order of Adam into disorder. Adam was designed to live and not ever die, and he was flawless, but the one thing Adam was not ready for was free will, and neither was I. If I were, I would not be in the situation that I am presently in. But only with mere words I waged war on Adam. I sometimes feel bad that I did this to poor Eve; she had nothing to do with my anger and jealously against Adam. I mean he was the one I was angry with, I did not want him to be created, that's all.

Why wouldn't you want God, or the King of Heavens, to create this Adam whom he wanted to exist?

I was just defending the good will and prosperity of the Angels of God. I was his Light Bearer. I was his Truth Keeper. How did I destroy my own position? How did I do this to my Legion and myself? Yes, it is a sad story, but the King of Heavens has a bazillion things happening at one time. You could never know what he's thinking, so I assumed he was only creating this one single Adam. I figured I could kill it, stop or delay the creation of it, but that did not work. In ignorance, I suggested to one-third of the Cherubs of my Legion to go along with my new plan, and not by the will of the King of Heavens, but what I wanted in my own heart.

Sir, is it not the King of Heaven's will for us to have and do the things we desire in our own hearts? So, all in all, people are still doing what he wills, in doing the things they desire to do correct?

You are absolutely wrong. The key words you used are, "things we desire in our own hearts." The things we want in our own hearts, this is what drives us all that have free will. The only species that exists, which perfectly follows what the King of Heavens wants, is the obedient Angels in Heaven above, and the animals, sea creatures, the bugs and weather patterns the King of Heavens created on this Earth. But again, as I thought about the King's will to create this Adam, I figured it would only be one. Since going back in my own memory, I jumped the gun. I became impatient and then I assumed this one Adam was going to live in Heaven above with us. Well, I must have only listened to half of the plan because the King later revealed he planned to create billions of these Adams. But that was a fault of mine, for which I am paying for to this day and forever until the King of Heavens comes down. My ability to tell the half of a truth and expand it to be believed by masses has gotten me into some deep judgment that I cannot escape. In the beginning, I was not like this. I can only remember the day I noticed my own covering, maybe? This is one-of-a-kind covering and that is another story. So, we rebelled against the Order of the King of Heavens and we were tossed out and down to this vile Earth due to our own hearts' desires instead of the King's will. That was a good misdirection, by the way.
(8 Isaiah 14:12-15)

Why thank you, I am still a professional, just doing my job.

So, back to the way I killed Adam, but still I didn't physically kill him, per se.

Interesting.

After Eve was relearning things from me, she was also learning how to suggest things, just like I did. It was a lovely thing. She was someone who listened to me, and even used my very own suggestions to confuse Adam to even covering himself with the same kinds of leaves I suggested from the Ghaf tree. The Word of the King of Heavens was walking on Earth, sometime after he had formed Adam for the King of Heavens, and Adam and The Word interacted; this happened now and then, but it began to be more sporadic. It seemed as if The Word was not around much, but this was a process to see how Adam would handle judgment alone. He was already highly intelligent enough to name all of the animals and creeping things of the entire Earth, which still have the same names he had given them to this very day, and all of the creations were concentrated in the region of Eden with the Adam placed directly in the center of this beginning that still has the same original animals and plants, and the very first strains of every plant and animal. Nowadays these new plants and animals are just a bunch of hybrids, cancer-causing plants and vegetation from tainted seeds of beasts and plants. Hey, but who am I?

Sir, this Word character; did he have a specific time he visited?

When The Word called forth to Adam on a certain sudden pop-up visit," just to see how things were going," lo and behold, I had gotten Eve to finally persuade Adam to wear a covering also. It was good that he had been practicing this for a while since the Eve convinced him, just as I did her. He listened to the suggestions, which were misleading, but they had a sense of sincerity behind them. "The Author of Confusion" title does fit perfectly. But since I could not physically kill Adam, I killed him from the inside out by deception. A little lie here and there, directly from the same one he was commanded not to speak to, or touch. Yet I get his wife to touch my covering and to listen to me and converse with me and she even confided in me. That was my revenge, my way of killing Adam. By making them change the simple order of The King of Heavens created for mankind and all things, with small suggestions over a period of time. I did this long enough until they believed they were making the decisions themselves. They made terrible decisions after my suggestions were placed, but it was a perfect plan for a long while for me. I had won the loyalty of the Fallen once more! Now they will work for me and not feel betrayed! Because in the beginning it was my suggestion that got us all ejected out of Heaven above. It was my fault, so I took the responsibility of getting us back into Heaven, and the only way to get back home is to destroy the creation of Adam.

Sir, by touching your covering, are you meaning you had carnal relations with the Eve you speak of?

I succeeded with destroying this creation by tainting its mindset. But the King of Heavens had a failsafe switch imbedded in the DNA of this man Adam that was passed down through his son Seth. Afterward, the King of Heavens reset Adam by this thing he called, "forgiveness of sins by sacrifice and repentance." He did not want to do it, but he had to show them the example of what death is. He made them remove the leaves and then he did something I have never before seen myself. The Word took the Hands of God and built an altar instantly. The altar was a perfect replica of the footstool of The Word, which he plants his feet on in his chamber room in Heaven. He commanded them bring each a choice heifer and a lamb and he killed them. This was the first time sacred blood was ever shed. He sprinkled the blood upon them and the altar and explained to them that they had to be cleansed while in the Garden. This blood of the heifer and lamb was to remind them that transgressing any instruction he gave them is equivalent to death.

(9 Genesis 3: 21-24)

Sir, what happened after the animals were killed?

The Word then commanded the skins of the animals be made into clothing and he covered Adam with the very animals he named. The same animals were his friends, because at this time of creation, all animals and things on this Earth spoke the same language. They communicated with Adam, all things of the air and waters and lands. They spoke to each other. That was a beautiful time for mankind and all kind. They were covered and clothed by The Word and led out by two cherubs who were my brethren, not as good looking as I am, but yes, they were very professional. He told them to go forth out of the garden and sent them away. Adam and Eve both now understood the purpose of their creation. They would procreate and produce more Gods to become the congregation of the Mighty God of Gods, King of Kings, and all rule with his first-born son, the Prince of Kings, The Word of God, his right hand. Adam was sent forth out of the garden, and he and Eve were led by two of my brethren; these are the two The Word has to stand on his left and right hand, blessed bastards. Adam and Eve also knew about the coming of Christ and his Armageddon as a result of any fault to be found in him. The revelation was even common knowledge to them. Adam knew since his falling away and having to start over, his children will forget The Word and purpose in which the Godhead created man.

Why does the whole World have to suffer because of Adam and Eve's faults? Why were they not discarded, and the King of Heavens just start over?

I will answer that one day. After Cain's generations, the whole Earth was getting ugly. The same way I did Adam, is the same way his children are doing to each other to this very day. The one thing that I finally figured out is what the King of Heavens was showing all of his creations. The knowledge, creation, and strength of Adam represented the King himself, and it was passed on to show what man can become; this was just the physical form or shape. The strength of the King of

Heavens and his Word began with Adam, and it appeared in Enoch, who perfected the knowledge of The King of Heavens, and was changed to be just as the King of Heavens, and has no appointed position until the thousand-year-rule of The Word, the Prince of Heavens. He will rule to correct all of mankind to steer them in the ways of the Kingdom of Heaven above.

Sir, you did not answer a few of my questions.

Through all of the generations of man, I have seen the strength of Adam displayed in three of these generations. The strength was seen in Jacob who was able to wrestle with one of the Holy Cherub angels from above for three days. This is unheard of, but I have seen it, this is another reason we had to help swiftly destroy them, if the seed of Jacob would be as many as it is written, these people would have accomplished the passing of the truth about the purpose of mankind through the laws of the Kingdom of Heaven above. How fair would that be for the seed of this man to be changed into something which is a natural body for us? Samson too displayed this strength greatly, yet I was able to make the strength of Samson sound as a fairytale to the entire World. If we did not corrupt or influence these people in any form or matter, they would have accomplished the goal of telling mankind their sole purpose. We sat at council and found out how to influence these seeds of Jacob, to further corrupt themselves and how to make them turn on each other. We Fallen have learned that the best way to destroy man is from the inside out and not the other way around. Again, the same procedure that was used to destroy Adam was applied, because the strength of Adam was found in Jacob. The last one who possessed the full power of the strength of Adam and the perpetual strength of the Godhead was The Word. I even tried to destroy his mission, which was to show man how to walk upright in his very own flesh according to the perfect laws and commands of the King of Heavens. The World literally knows how all of that went. It was the first time I was directly rejected and if I just could have accomplished that mission, then we Angels would have had a chance to exist in this celestial form even longer.

You tried to stop the one who came as the Christ, and what is the difference between he and Adam?

This is the difference between the First Adam and the Second Adam which is The Word, the Prince of the King of Heavens, who came to show man how to walk in the image he was given, called flesh, to be changed to eternal Celestials as the King of Heavens desires. He did not make it complicated or difficult to reach this goal. I had to make it seem difficult to expand my time in this beautiful body of mine. By following the Second Adam is the literal way to become an eternal Celestial. But what we did not account for was this strength; it was distributed evenly amongst the ones that were scattered throughout the entire World in the fulfillment of the prophecy, by The Word. Nowadays, we do not know when or if the strength will be displayed amongst humans again, but we speculate it will be in the two witnesses who will go against the man of perdition, this will be my grand finale and stand.

Okay sir, what have you been up to these *present* days?

I do not have much to do nowadays, except give suggestions to whosoever wants my suggestions and influence. There is no guarantee they will get away with the acts of evil at all. None, not even a percentage of a fraction, shows them getting away with the ill deeds I suggest. I do not offer forgiveness, or good resolutions, I give them illusions to make it seem as though no consequence will be paid. For every bad action, word, and thought of man or Celestial will be answered for in the day of judgment by the King of Heavens himself at the very last day. There is still one final kingdom to rise on Earth. It will be left to rule for one thousand years before his Majesty the King of Heavens arrives. This may be too much for you to handle or fathom. You mere humans are just dumb Adamites who do not even realize that even at fifty years old you are just in a cocoon stage of your existence. If I only knew back then what I know now is just wishful thinking presently, but decisions had to be made.

(10 1Peter 5:6-8)

So do you know what the *original* sin of man is?

After The Word called Adam forth and he hid himself, it was because he knew the very First Commandment he received was not to listen to, touch, or go near, no other than me. I was the tree in the middle of the garden. I love how you Adamites cannot comprehend The Word, even when he had it written in a book for all of you. It is simply amazing how you cannot catch this novice notion. Most of you Adamites are too busy trying to go to Heaven above by murders, deaths, suicides, and doctrines. How can you go to Heaven above when you are not from Heaven above, neither were you ever promised to go to Heaven above? The only ones who desire to go to Heaven above are myself and the one-third of the Fallen Angels who want to go home, away from this decaying rock, this putrid and vile place filled with walking fleshly animals and people. We are not from here! Disobedience is the original sin of mankind!

Sir, how long have you been "imprisoned" on the Earth?

Millennia! So many millennia! We existed before you! How can you get a higher promise in the Kingdom of the King of Heavens than we do! I still cannot wrap my mind around that. You will have the ability to be like him, you will have a higher position than me, who was created first? I was the first-born of the Angels of God. It was me who was first of the Cherubs, the most powerful Angels—do you not realize this? Your home is not in Heaven above, it is the Earth, do you not understand? The same exact place the King of Heavens desires to live. This damned place. Who would want to live here? Why would my great King want to live here?

(11 Ezekiel 28:1-4, 11-19; Isaiah 11:1-5, 9-10)

So, if you could, what would you change? Or what would you do?

I want to go back home and I will rule above all the Sons of God, and even God himself! I am the one who wants to go home! I figured out how to kill all of the sons of Adam, simply by making them follow me. Isaiah told you about me, but you did not listen. You thought it was all a bunch of mumbo jumbo. When you bury your dead, they are simply sleeping. But I taught you that they perish and go to Heaven above. This is how I kill many members of mankind, simply by suggestions and by their own lusts of power. Sometimes it is so funny because each and every time, you children of the First Adam fall for the same exact things in each generation. The possibilities that one of you will fall off and become wicked are very high, because you all come from the same blood of the Adam and Eve. The bad decisions of Adam and naive mind of Eve both combined in you all makes it easy to defer you, even during the simplest choices. The Adamites were given power and dominion over all the animals on the Earth, the fowl, creeping things, and the fish and animals of the seas. That power was given to you to be an example of what the Kingdom of Heaven should be, according to his Laws and Order at his arrival, to be a good Kingdom of judges of things that are, and that are to come. But through years of lies, I was able to slow this process down.

(12 Daniel 7:26-27)

Sir, who all knew of these things you speak of? How many of them are they?

The Word and the King are the only two who know of the full capabilities, and even his purpose for everything. This is why The Word was chosen for the job to take the Hands of God, and the leagues of Cherubs and Terrapins and create.

(13 John 1:1-3, 10-12, 15; Job 38:1-13, 18; Psalms 33:4-9, 12-15; Isaiah 45:18-22; Genesis 1:1-7, 26-27)

Sir, I remember you mentioning children? Who are your children? Is Nimrod the only one?

Yes, Nimrod was my first born of many who came after him in the flesh. I had to figure out a way to exist, a way to keep my tradition and my image alive. I had to truly think about this thing I was about to perform. I could not fathom how I could earn back the trust of the Fallen Legion, but at the same time lie to them, because we all knew that whatever the King of Heavens and His Word has put forth it will come to pass no matter what and there is nothing one can do. I figured out a way to, per se, buy us some time. Since we know that the rebellion was caused by us, there is no forgiveness for that act. With that fact known, I simply made the suggestion to just corrupt every single human born on Earth so we can extend our existence in this celestial form we were given. In the case of The Word of God, as it is written in the Holy Scrolls, man will become a celestial being, if, having kept the ordinances of God, through the humbleness of Christ. Then each and every person born on this entire planet would be able to live forever in the oneness of the King of Heavens and The Word. My Angels and I set out to corrupt the World through religions we_created and gave each group and subgroup of humans a god or savior. We had to move fast because we had realized we lost lots of time due to the gap of time between the death of Eve and the birth of Nimrod. If we did not make a move, the end of our existence as true celestial beings would have been over at an earlier stage of mankind's history. After the first Nimrod, we made many Nimrods, one in each country and in each tongue, and in every mind of each and every human born in each generation. We also added the concept of government to mimic the perfect government of the King of Heavens. This task was worthy only because it bought us more time to feel the power in this body of perfection. Since our fall during the rebellion, we had to make decisions. We, too, would not have the same body at the end of the last stage of the Adamites. Even we Angels who sinned against the King will be transformed into something different, and placed in eternal damnation, in the Great Lake of Undying Fire and Brimstone that burns forever and ever. All of the Adamites who have sinned against the King of Heavens will also be transformed and placed into the same Great Lake of Fire and Brimstone.

(14 Revelation 20:11-15; Isaiah 66:15-18, 23-24; Matthew 24:29-31, 35-39, 43-44; Matthew 25:31-34, 41)

So, you are telling me that instead of facing your punishment for a transgression you initiated, you decided to kill all humans so you could live in your eternal body just a few moments longer?

Of course, we hate humans. The Legion had to act fast because the King had already placed an expiration date on the Adamites. The King allowed the Adamites seven of his days to get themselves prepared mentally for the Kingdom of Heaven which will be placed on this Earth forever. The King has always had his heart set on this planet, since before the actual creation. So, the Fallen of our Legion had a council just as we did in the third heaven when we used to meet with the King of Heavens each morning and sang to the King and his Prince. It sounds insane, but we still do our best to mimic the ordinances of the Kingdom we were kicked out of to this planet. Each and every move we try to make, is to be just as the Godhead, because it is the only order that works. The very baffling part of it all is the fact that, as intelligent as we Cherubs are, we still cannot level with the thoughts of the Elohim, the King of Heaven and His Word the_Prince. We have been around longer than man and cannot phantom as to why man, or we, have not accomplished creating anything through the carnal Earth and its soil as he has done. We know the measurements, the math, the hours and time it takes to create man, plants, and animals; we witnessed him creating everything. We know exactly how to do things with this carnal Earth, but we are always missing some element and we cannot figure out what it is. We still strive to live as kings and rulers amongst men in the gore and carnage we created by our rebellion and my deception to Eve, to the destruction of the first Adam.

How could you be viewed as good if you destroy?

We had to use these tactics to mimic the King of Heaven's order. It is impossible without him and we have tried everything to duplicate all of his order, but in this carnal world and mindsets of humans it cannot bring forth good works. I feel my job of extending the time of my Legion of Angels has been a very good run. No human could have done what I have done. No human could have caused the damage I have done. I have destroyed you all, even those who do not believe. I have touched their lives in many matters, and they do not realize that I have ruled their lives from their birth up until present day.

How have you destroyed everyone, sir?

You do not destroy the children of Adam by a gigantic lie or story of falsehoods. No, you destroy them with small spoons of a good and tasty lie; one that is directed to man's very own self-obsessions and conceits. You do this through pride, through self-absorption; pride in things that man does not own, the very soil each foot in the World stands on. They do not realize that the land they stand on, even the seas and the abysses, the very air this man breathes, belongs to the King of Heavens and The Word His Prince. Man was just a custodian to the World, to take care of it until the appointed time.

What are you to do before the appointed time?

Our job to extend our time comes from the great ability of man to pass down traditions from generation to generation. If man would have been able to pass down the ways of the King of Heavens and The Word his Prince to each of their generations, man would have been in the regeneration ages ago and would already become what he was designed to be. Man would not be flesh and blood but the Celestial, just and perfect, and duplicated in the image of the King of Heavens and The Word his Prince.

There are *thousands* of traditions in the realm of traditions, cultures, and peoples. Are you saying you gave the World its *different traditions?*

I did the same thing the King of Heavens did, but opposite. I gave you an anti-messiah, and instead of giving a single one, I gave you many because it would be harder to track the source back to Nimrod and, of course, me. We had to create many a religion from our main source Babylonian. Directly from the Kingdom of Babel comes all confusion from religion to government. Babel means confusion and, well, Babylonia is a government of confusions which I created, and again the King of Heavens slaps me in the face by having it written in the scrolls that I am the author of confusion. It was easy for me to take the true words of the tablets and change their meanings, just as it was easy for me to influence men to rebel and kill each other over trinkets and precious rocks of the Earth. These same wretched rocks that cover my celestial body are yet invisible to mankind.

You are saying that no one has ever seen you, but all the while you are sitting here in an interview with me?

The only way man can see me is willingly, but I will not appear unless the blood of one they love is sacrificed.

Is killing their loved one the *only* way to see you?

It has to be that way; what if they change their minds? That would not be any fun. Following me comes with a price. I give them carnal riches and pleasures beyond their wildest imaginations. They become my children given to me by my first born, Sin.

So you are telling me that every rich or wealthy person is your follower and child?

It is not a doubt and a fact that anyone can have wealth by following the order of the King of Heavens, but righteousness is so easy, being good and following the King of Heavens is very simple. But it is as the children nowadays say, lame? Or whatever the latest term is. Following an order to become the sons and daughters of the King of Heavens to be judges of all things is not good enough for the Adamites. I give very temporary riches, which the simple-minded Adamites absolutely love. The Adamites follow my child, my prince, Sin. Sin makes them fornicate in every way imaginable from fleshly lusts to theft to worship of false gods, who are no more than just my alter egos.

You mentioned that you are afraid of the Great Lake of Fire and Brimstone; how could this hurt you if you are an Angel?

What could an Angel be changed into? In this Great Lake of Fire and Brimstone, what could a Fallen Angel possibly be changed into? I do not know what this final form for evildoers is. The Fallen and the disobedient Adamites will both be changed into something that can never die but can feel pain and suffer forever by burning with fire and brimstone and never to disintegrate. Even during the burning and screaming there will be flesh eating worms that do not die from the fire. They will be able to eat away at this undying body of eternal destruction, and this form will be burned and eaten at forever and never being completely devoured. This body seems to heal at an accelerated rate and burn and die every day. The body seems to be a combination of the celestial and the terrestrial body that will be imprisoned forever with no ability to move, or escape, absolutely no mercy will suffice for the rest of eternity.

You seem to be terrified of this place? Where is this place located?

The location of this payment for disobedience will be in the badlands of the Kingdom on Earth. To remind all generations of the last Adamites who will be redeemed in the Earthly Kingdom of The Word in the

Seventh Day. This body was not discussed, until after the death of Isaiah. It was not revealed to the Fallen that this is the second death. We have made a terrible mistake, but we are still willing to eternally kill all of the Adamites we possibly can. We will not stop, though we know the price for our works. We will still kill as many of you bastards as we can by our suggestions, even if it means experiencing physical pain for the first time in our lives and then forever, we will go the extra mile because we absolutely hate you Adamites

Why thank you, sir, for your time and effort answering all of these grueling questions. Our staff will provide you with hot meals and any beverages you please. Take a hot shower, get relaxed and get you some rest in the comfortable bed provided. We will review all of your answers and a case worker will be with you in the morning to figure out what steps we will take going forward in your case. Have a great night, sir.

...and God called the firmament Heaven. And the evening and the morning were the **Second Day**.

Agent: Good morning sir, how are you and what is today?

Today, well of course, it is the second day of the week.

Agent: Today is the first day of the week, sir. Monday.

No, contrary to what you believe, the fact is today is Monday, the second day of the week. If you dare to look at the Western wall of this room, and proceed to read to me the days of the week according to the calendar that is pinned on the wall, you will understand that today is the second day of the week. Monday. Be sure to read from left to right.

The interviewer peered to his right and looked at the calendar. He did a double-take and swallowed his very own pride.

FEBRUARY 2025						
S	M	T	W	T	F	S
						1
2	3	4	5	6	7	8
9	10	11	12	13	14	15
16	17	18	19	20	21	22
23	24	25	26	27	28	

Agent: Lesson learned, knowledge earned. How was your sleep and what is on your mind this *second* day of the week?

Well, I never slept if it matters to you, but it was good to give you that early morning zinger of facts; even you cannot deny the truth of it.

Agent: You did not sleep one single wink?

*No, there is no need to, why would an eternal being need to sleep? I am merely trapped in this body for a short period of time. You have exactly up until the **seventh** day to get all of the information you think you can get from me. On the seventh day, decisions will be made with all 2,300 persons in this entire facility's boundaries, lives are at stake. But as far as what is on my mind, I was thinking about the big invasion that will come upon the Earth.*

Agent: Interesting; when is this big invasion? Elaborate, please.

The big invasion, the day the unseen will materialize in front of your very eyes one day soon, which is shortly after my son Nimrod is resurrected.

Agent: How can *you* resurrect Nimrod who is *dead*? He has been dead for ages.

There are many forms of spirit. Words are spirit, one. The air you breathe is spirit, two. The mindsets, thoughts, and the way you think, three. Then there are Holy and evil Angels, four. I just showed you four forms of what defines spirit, out of its many forms. I said all of that so you may understand that my son Nimrod is not dead. Yes, he is physically dead, but his spirit or his mindset, his way of thinking, lives on in this world. The mind of Nimrod that became dedicated to my purposes has never died. The great hour of temptation is nearing and I will see my son physically manifested in a new mindset of a person that will be even more powerful than the original one.

Agent: What makes the *new* Nimrod more powerful than the first one?

The new mindset, the new way of thinking, will engulf the entire Earth and then all will be for me for a possession for a time. The hour of temptation is Great Tribulations he will bring upon this Earth for 1,260 days. In those days my son Nimrod will rule in my stead. I will be his god that gives him all the power to do some peculiar miracles, to persuade followers to think he is God or even the son of the True God. But he is my son, my loyal follower who will deceive the nations of this entire World to follow my will. There will be death to those who despise my mark to buy and sell, and to those who will not abide in the traditions I gave you all. The traditions I gave men will bound them forever to the Lake of Eternal Fire, their precious traditional celebrations will connect them with the flames forever.

Agent: How can anyone avoid such things you speak about in a *time* that has *not* come, and what does one do to protect themselves and their families?

You Adamites are simpletons. You all claim that you have a god in all of the religious settings I gave you, but I never answer the many repetitious prayers that are chanted each day. You do not simply understand what the Godhead mindset is like or what even comes close to it, nor do any of you really want to understand. How can you ask about protection for yourself when you do not even care to try to understand a fragment of the mind of the one who created all things? You never want to follow him, so I gave you all many options to follow, the things and traditions you wanted to covet instead. I gave you absolutely nothing.

Agent: What is this *Godhead* mindset you are speaking about? Can it help protect one from your new Nimrod?

The mindset of God is as this, you have a central source of power that flows through the celestial. That power is coming from the King's Eternal Godhead and through his word to all. If you want to live forever you have to become a part of that central source of power. If you are not part of the central mindset, you are not a part of that central connection of power that changes you into what it is. Having any flaw in your mindset will get you cut off from the perfect way. It is totally a change of mind. You cannot have anything that is against the flow of the Godhead. Your mind must be willing to be all good, and according to his way, and his way of understanding is simply obedience. You must walk the path he has given you and you will be just like him in the end. Having the mindset of God is like this. Take, for example, if you could almost sum up the mind of God, it could simply be that you would have all power, you would be the perfect good, the sum total of being a great leader, and the beginning of all things.

Agent: Is this all we need to know about the Godhead you are speaking of? Is there any other detrimental information we "Adamites" need to know about your presumed God of all? It simply seems that you are fear mongering, or just in fear of something that may not be real.

The Godhead mindset is not limited at all for the understanding of the purpose of his Word, the Prince of all things. Every great king has a great prince to carry out his will. The Word is that great Prince who works constantly up until the final day of rest. This is also a great portion to know, so that you may understand the Eternal Godhead. The fear you speak of is just merely the fear of man, as you flesh bags always think immediately because you are ignorant. Fear of the King and his Prince is the detrimental information you need to know and understand if you plan on missing his judgment upon all of mankind both dead and alive. Many will die in this very brief war to come on this Earth.

Agent: If I may interrupt, you are telling me that humans need to be *absolutely* afraid of *your* God. Not anything else on Earth but *your* God?

My God? Did you just say, my God? He is not just my God, my King, and my Creator. He is yours and all things in which you see and cannot see. He is the God of all things. Did you not understand, that I literally just said, the fear you speak of is just merely the fear of man, as you flesh bags always think immediately, because you are ignorant? I just told you these things minutes ago and you completely ignored it. Again, I simply proved all of you Adamites are just ignorant. Fear is knowing who you are dealing with, fear is understanding that the King of Heavens and his Prince the Word are the only two Gods which exist at this present time. Fear is knowing the end of mankind's existence. Fear is knowing the Gospel and return of the King's Word to the Earth. Fear is obeying the commands and laws of the King of Heavens in which he gave all to live by. Fear is treating fellow beings as your very own brethren, because you are. Fear is simply defined as obedience to the King of Heaven by the ordinances he created and lives by even himself. For the eternities he and his Prince have always existed in, it has been, Obedience is the key to perfect fear of God.

Agent: Who do you fear? Because the actions you have told me do not line up with the words you are expressing.

I fear the King of Heavens and his Word, yet I keep hope that I can defeat them both and show the counsel of the Heavens that the King was wrong in his decision to create mankind. Once they see he is wrong, I can beat them by voting them out by force. They will be forced to stand in judgment by their own laws, for creating such an atrocious being who is bent on killing itself from all existence. I can watch from the Heaven above from the same throne room and **court** *I was kicked out of and watch mankind kill themselves, especially for the bywords they have called me for ages. I hate Adamites, and I hate this kingdom.*

Agent: Is one of your goals for killing mankind due to the fact that they call you names? It sounds like you are the one who caused your own issues, yet you are blaming someone else for your shortcomings. Yet, how can you want to destroy everything, and also be a ruler, simply because someone called you a name or criticized your actions?

Have you ever been called something that is not of your character or description? The accuser has never seen you, or met you, but they have great opinions of you? Have you been made into some uncivilized caricature of an Adamite idea? Drawn by something that cannot even comprehend the King of Heavens or his Word, yet it has the audacity to spew words and images of defamation to the beauty of your entire legacy?

Agent: No. Not any events I can recall to this day.

Your winners of beauty pageants, and constant feats of carnal competition, could not compare to a speckle of my beauty. I was created by special order of the King of Heavens. You have no perception of beauty—this is one of the main reasons I want to destroy all of you Adamites. I fight for many reasons, but to call one a devil, Satan, Beelzebub, demon, lord of Hades, king of the underworld, ugly and gruesome, is the worst thing any of you Adamites could have ever done. Now you have turned my beauty into a mere mockery.

Agent: Sir, are you saying that you hate satanic art pieces? This seems to be the message I am getting.

I see myself as a freedom fighter from the revolution of this God who wants to make a non-celestial into a celestial. The one title I can hold onto is the Prince of the Power of the Air! All of the other titles are just terrible and not fitting of a beautiful prince such as me. I am one of a kind, priceless; so the name is fitting to me.

Agent: Which name, sir?

You know, the Prince of the Power of the Air. I especially admire this title because, with this power, I can control emotions and give people that are located anywhere different suggestions, from anywhere on the planet. I mean, why should I limit myself from the war technology I helped influence across this entire Earth?

Agent: Which war technologies did you influence, sir? Do share.

I influenced all war technology from every period of history since the existence of man since Adam. All. If I were to share it all with you, you would reconsider everything you have ever been taught as being a lie.

Agent: Ok. Do you mind sharing how you control people's emotions?

I control emotions through the airwaves. Anything, which can create airwaves or is connected to the airwaves, I can control it and I just speak my suggestions through the waves. I can suggest through any wave that passes through land, sea, and air and that is the whole Earth.

Agent: That is all for today, sir.

The agent became a little frustrated because he felt that his efforts, though genuine, were being mocked by the subject. He sighed, slowly closed his notepad, stood up and walked out. The door shut behind the interviewer and the man sat there alone in the room, sitting on the couch. He sat still and very quiet for a few minutes, then he crossed his legs and spread his arms across the back of the couch he sat on.

For almost two days I have been asked questions and I have responded to each of the questions I have been given. You and I are attached for a reason and I don't know why just yet, I will allow you to speak, but my question to you is when am I able to ask you a few questions?

Even though I am terrified. You can ask me any questions you would like to. There is no harm in asking questions.

Good. What is your response to the question of man and his purpose for existence?

I would respond and say man is from Heaven above, and man's only existence is to die; to make it to the kingdom of Heaven above. The Bible tells us so, why do you think *all* religions talk about going to Heaven above? Yes, we all have the same God, we just *view* him *differently*. We all have the ability to get to Heaven above; it's just a matter of where your heart is. Jesus is the way, and all we have to do is just believe on his name and we shall be saved. That is John 3:16, for God so loved the World, that he gave his only begotten Son, that whosoever believeth in him should not perish, but have everlasting life.

I have a question: doesn't John 14:15 say, if ye love me, keep my commandments?

Well, that has nothing to do with John 3:16, or 1ˢᵗ Thessalonians 4:17, we will be evermore with the Lord, he directly tells us through the letters of The Apostle Paul, that we will be in Heaven. We will be with him. You know you cannot get past the truth of the word of *God*. You know the dead in Christ are in Heaven above!

Why does it clearly say in Genesis 2:7, man, the First Adam, was made a LIVING SOUL? You radiant man of intelligence; you are the soul. It is also written in Genesis, from dust thou art to dust thou shalt return. I see you don't read where it is written that even the man after the King of Heaven's own heart, David, is even dead and buried today in the sepulchers of the Kings. So how are you going to Heaven above, my friend? Even the one named Moses did not go to Heaven above. I truly tried to get that body; if I would have gotten it. I could have bought even more time. But the King of Heavens commanded it be hidden until the resurrection of the dead, the regeneration. How dare you boast to the one who gave you this doctrine you grotesquely spit?

So by your analogies you talk against the rapture? This is why I know you are lying! You speak against the rapture of God in Heaven to be with him forever! How could such a blasphemous demon be attached to me? Why do you lie?

It is very obvious I have taught you well. I have taught you to stand solid on the principles I put forth that are contrary to what the eternal tables have said. I have successfully taught you to believe and to teach what I have put forth in this World. First, let me educate you a little further. The rapture is merely a bit of wishful thinking of mine that I incorporated into mainstream religions all over the planet. Yes, each religion has a main theme of going to Heaven above. But it is easily seen by experts amongst you, that it is the Fallen and I who wish to go home to Heaven, and we laced this theme throughout the World through religions. The rapture is just a representation of the trillions upon trillions (just so I won't blow your mind) of the one-third of Fallen Angels who wish and long to go home, but we cannot ever return. I thought it was hilarious that even my deepest wish was written in the scrolls of the prophets. It is written in the scroll of Isaiah that I want to go home to Heaven and rule above the King of Heaven. It states every detail of my innermost thoughts which no one knew. Even when I thought to be king over all the Angels of Heaven, to be like the highest existence, the King of Heavens, that very secret thought of mine was written. To buy more time, I developed a basic theology to give to the World; I told them that one dies and goes to Heaven, instead of man is appointed to die once with the hopes of being raised into forevermore. I made my ministers associate death with going to Heaven above, no matter what form of death became a person. Death and afterwards going to Heaven above is something that cannot be proven by men, something untraceable, something that can be driven by sorrow mixed with pure belief of a fallacy. Only when the person themselves can step away from this falsehood, can they realize that no one has reported back to say everything is well. A logical person sees the simplicity of the Word of The King of Heavens, but I have saturated the World with a fantasy of the Fallen, a mere myth even amongst Angels. The theology of the World's churches comes from me. The way this happens is, every trait of my theology exists in each religion. Some settings may not be as saturated with as many images and signs and doctrines as the next, but what is understood is that a little leavening leavens the whole lump. If I can input one or two blasphemies along with watered-down words of truth, then this could buy me time. Again, the goal is to teach the children of Adam and all offspring the ways that are against God, so that we may prolong our Celestial form, to delay man from becoming Celestials, and at the same time decreasing the numbers of them which could easily obtain this new body and way of life eternal. We know that the Kingdom of Heaven will be here on Earth and we had to think of a clever way to defer this fact from the Children of Adam. We just reversed everything and spread rumors to make the Word of God a burden to men, and by setting up our own ministers on a global scale. Globalization is not merely goods, services, products, and technology, it is also the spreading of particular words, attitudes, and beatitudes that can be programmed into each and every person on Earth. There are many ways each and every human connects, and we figured out how to breach that connect and make it a global fall. We continue pushing the fallacies, stressing them through our ministers who sit at the head of each of these organizations, and we reward them with vile pleasures.

Mankind loves all kinds of fleshly things, so it can be very easily perverted among those who follow the Fallen and teach men our doctrines by mere suggestions of persuasion. They do it for power, fiat, and lusts, some like children and they are grotesque, and will do every manner of evil to please us. The irony is that man has the ability to overturn all of the lies we, the Fallen, have put forth. Again, you don't have the capacity to understand that man was designed to live forever. The very blaspheme you scream is the same way I taught you to rebel against the King of Heavens. Even when I tell you the source of your very own belief, you are ready to debate with a being that is more powerful than you and knows more than you. The very evil which created your belief is telling you where it comes from, the very source of your disobedience is telling you how to change, and you even try to rebut the creator of your confusion. I have to keep laughing at mankind because out of all creations you are the most stubborn lovers of the evils of the carnal mind and carnal flesh. The god of lies and material possessions, the one who seeks to destroy you, is telling you how to overcome the falsehoods I taught you. Even as I have confessed to teaching you wrong, you still love the evil I gave you, just as the scrolls have said. The scrolls and tables have not ever lied. The direct orders of the King of Heavens by the Word, his Prince.

The people behind the glass wall had a short meeting after the exchange between the subject and what seemed to be someone else, some other personality, or something else. The interviewer and observers witnessed this spine-chilling conversation unfold, which made many re-think their first round of findings.

Agent: How could such an ancient spirit be attached to this man? The objective of this being is very clear. It is claiming it is the adversary written in the Bible, correct? He or it refers to the scrolls or the tables and what is written on them. So it is plain to see there is suspected to be some sort of end-time jargon being thrown around, because this is oddly strange and, according to the recorded transcripts and reviewing the words and references this "Alien'" is using, it clearly is quoting the Bible.

Officer: I wonder why it is only quoting the Bible and not any other ancient texts? Maybe you can incorporate this in your session, maybe todays or in the future?

Agent: I will most definitely add this new information into my future conversations according to the timeframe he has given us.

Officer: His body is at a nuclear level, but the body is

unharmed. We are having a hard time comprehending this entity that has somehow kept the body alive and, literally, has not melted the specimen into watered-down gelatin. Face recognition tech has identified Jude Brownstone as the specimen we have in custody. His file has been uploaded into the system. You can view the information we have on him from your device, of course.

Agent: What's even more amazing is the fact that I have not had a trace of radiation poisoning or any kind of sudden cancers. Sir, I am going to go in there and do my very best. This situation can finally answer a lot of questions about us being the only ones in this galaxy or the entire universe.

Officer: E.A.R.T.H. is counting on you, and the Earth is, too. This is very serious.

The agent nods his head and stands, then leaves the room after shaking the hand of the officer in charge of the investigation. As he walks down the hallway for a few meters, down the dark and gloomy area passing the office of the OIC (officer in charge), he thinks about how he might interject the things he needed when interviewing the subject, Jude Brownstone. There had to be something that he could do, in order to accomplish the task he aimed to finish.

He arrived home in the early evening a few hours before sundown. He sat in his midsize apartment at the computer checking emails about urgent and non-urgent matters. He sipped on some fine wine and played tunes by Earth, Wind and Fire, and many various other extinct forms of music which were now banned by most of the World's governments, but readily available and free in the resorts and space cabin getaways of the Space Frontier Elite Separatists (SFES). He closed his eyes, grooved to the music, and enjoyed the simple but euphoric feelings each sip of wine delightfully delivered with the smell, the texture, and the weightlessness that the perfectly aged grapes consistently brought forth from each bottle. His mind raced on the prior events at E.A.R.T.H. with this special subject with a suspicion of paranoia, schizophrenia, or could it be paranormal activity?

This new task can help many and answer so many questions if it is done correctly and not in the very order it has always been done. The old way is to destroy what we do not understand, infiltrate, befriend, learn all abilities and weaknesses, use the resources for mission fulfillment, and finally destroy with all prejudices. This time, if done right, we can simply fulfill the curiosity everyone on Earth has always had all their lives about aliens and their existence, or their wonders about the paranormal and unseen. Ever since he saw the first documents of the Roswell crash landing, he sought to find out if this ever happened; was it a government cover-up, or is it something else going on that humanity is just not cognizant of? Is this a phenomenon that mankind has no idea of how to "see" or access? Is there a way for mankind to know these things, and is the way to learn about all of the paranormal, all of the unseen" Is the key to all of this within the walls of E.A.R.T.H.? There is only one way to find out and that is simply to ask the right questions. The right questions could get the results that would help humanity understand

these kinds of strange things that happen in the World. But if this is not
something that can help, it is a waste of precious time that could have
been put into something else, and we are left with an unknown nuclear
risk. It is time to find out; it is time someone does something.

He stared at the horizon as the sun went down at 7:30PM to
begin a new day, and he continued to sip the best wine and snack
on a few leftovers he had in the refrigerator before turning in to bed.

…And the earth brought forth grass, and herb yielding seed
after his kind, and the tree yielding fruit, whose seed was in itself,
after his kind: and God saw that it was good. And the evening and
the morning were the **Third Day**.

The agent entered the door and found the subject sitting upright
and in the same position he left him in yesterday. He seemed a bit
shook up, but responsive and willing to talk.

Hello Mr. Brownstone, how are you this morning?

I'm doing OK this morning. But, am I insane? Or is something
really attached to me or inside of me? Can you please tell me
something because I'm really beginning to freak out because I have
never been through anything like this. Yes, I have done all kinds of
drugs in my wandering, but nothing like this. What is going on?

Don't worry, sir, a few more sessions and we can get to the
bottom of all this. I'm sure if we keep up the good work we will
get to the very bottom of this mystery. We have applied the
proper approach to this kind of situation, sir. Mr. Brownstone,
I guarantee you that by all means we will do our very best to
help you walk away from this unscathed.

I hope so, because I don't know how long I can deal with this.

This is just as stressful as losing my family! I don't know if I can bare this.

The agent put his hand on Mr. Brownstone's shoulder, and reassured him with strong concern and a beam of hope that they would somehow get through this. That they will end this in the time appointed.

Hey, let's get through this together. If you would have a seat we can get started. The more each day passes the closer we are to the deadline which he has given us. This is one deadline I do not want to miss. Oddly, the unknown scares me, especially the ones with possibilities. I'm going to have a seat and you can lie on the couch or whatever is comfortable for you.

Good doctor you didn't even tell me good morning. I was listening the entire time. I mean, I thought we were developing a relationship?

No, sir, I have not forgotten about you, just a mere misunderstanding. I was just speaking to the first person that was available. I apologize if I seemed a bit rude.

Modest answer.

Shall we continue?

Yes, yes sir, we can.

They take their places and the entity allowed the subject to lie on the couch to get comfortable. Mr. Brownstone, for the first time in this strange situation which was like a lucid dream, was able to relax and be himself without the stress of thinking he was insane. He was able to get comfortable in the manner he liked and to get a little steam off his chest caused by this experience he seemed to be going through.

If I may ask, are you, too, ready to continue, sir?

I am ready, I just want you to know that the King of Heavens and his Word only deals with Kings. We will arrive at this conclusion later, isn't that right Agent O? Since you know his name, at least let him know your alias.

…And the evening and the morning were the **Third day**.

Agent O: What is something that bothers you presently, or has bothered you in the past?

> *There are many things on this earth, which has bothered me in the past, and yet there are things, that presently makes me abhor Adamites.*

Agent O: Do you mind sharing?

> *Of course not, any platform to express my excellent hatred of Adamites, I am always willing to expound on. The present day thing that bothers me is the argument of the flat earth versus the round earth. This is only one of the most ignorant things you humans have come up with in the last century. How can either side of you have a debate, to know what this earth is shaped like? How could a being which is capable of lying to each other; with space hoaxes, programs, television and movies, to build up a false sense of everything that exists, even have a fragment of a clue of the form of the entire earth? The most hilarious part of it all is that I am the one who even gave you this suggestion to believe*

these things, and in your ignorance, you are worshipping me because I am the one who suggested these things to be done.

Agent O: Interesting, do you mind sharing more?

All of my wishes have been executed perfectly for a very long time, yet even I have a time to cease to rule. Man is not capable to fly into the depths of outer space; the King of Heavens will not allow him. He is earthy, from the earth; no human will ever get beyond the firmament to the third heaven. No man is ever allowed in this realm of the Kingdom of Heaven. Man can only access the first and second heavens.

Agent O: So is the earth flat or round?

It is merely whatever shape you believe it can be; whatever possibility of a form you can conceive in thought. Just know that there are seven continents and an endless supply of waters within waters that go deeper and higher than you can perceive. Ones imagination can run wild in this instance but just know that the shape of the world you live in is no kind of shape or domed world or any imagination mankind has to offer, only celestials can comprehend what you call the shape of this world and the entire galaxies which the King of Heaven designed in a mere fragment of a thoughts thought.

Agent O: Can it also be, a diamond type of shape? I perceive it to be a diamond.

Yes, it is one of many quadrillions of ideas and thoughts of how many perceive the planet to be shaped.

Agent O: So the earth is not flat?

The earth is not flat. Mankind has lied to each other for so long on many aspects of life that it is easy to manipulate each

and every one of you to believe whatever I want you to. The
Cushites is the only ones who acquired the knowledges of the
signs of the heavens, and the perfect maths and sciences in
which they even figured out that the earth was indeed round.
All knowledge is not good knowledge, but knowledge with
wisdom and understanding is the best thing, I never taught with
wisdom and understanding, or anything of good knowledge.
Just remember a key fact is, All of my children listen to me.

Agent O quickly took some more notes as the subject seemed very confident in his answer.

Agent O: Do you have any children?

Yes, I have a son. He has long been dead
now, about seven thousand years.

Agent O: Do you mind if we talk about him?

No, he was a great warrior in my book. He understood my
will. That is why I will bring him back in the end.

Agent O: How could you bring him back, if you did not create man?

Easily, he will be reincarnated spiritually. He will sit where I will
command him and rule this vile world to its destruction.

Agent O: How can you bring him back spiritually as you just mentioned?

If thou therefore wilt worship me, the entire world shall be yours.
Those were the first words I spoke to him. I had many suggestions he
freely went along with, though he knew the suggestions I gave him were
absolutely wrong. This is when I found the flaw in the Adams' genus.

Agent O: What happened after you found the "flaw" so to speak?

This was the moment I was able to taint the entire creation of the generations of Adam, and end this silly creation. I fully implemented the myth of going to heaven above, through the enforcements of Nimrod with the power and riches I gave him. Every single thing your fathers of earth have taught you until this present day is the same words I have given them through Nimrod. I only told him exactly what I wanted to do. Today my exact words is taught and is passed down from Nimrod, to all generations by ways of religions and theologies in the which, I created and influenced on an interplanetary scale. I also gave you all of my images to worship in the form of the sun.

Agent O: You are the inventor of every religion on the planet? You implemented these systems as you claim?

Of course, why do you think you are told at funeral proceedings that the deceased has made their transition to heaven above or reincarnation occurs? You carnal minded imbeciles cannot even comprehend what is going on. Every Adamite is just like the older versions of itself; you do not read to understand the logic of creation or what it means to be a creator. This flaw has been in your DNA matrix since the first Adam. How can your kind be in heaven above?

Agent O: How do you feel about mankind being in heaven or near it?

How does your kind deserve heaven above? How can your kind believe that you absolutely, do not have to do any kinds of works to receive the reward of the eternal? Insanity! When have you ever worked a 9 to 5, for 365 days of the year in a job or career and not expect to get your pay for the terms in which you and your employer agreed to?

*Of course not! What I gave you, was the idea. The idea of something being **similar** to something in any form, is not the exact same thing.*

Agent O: That is true, one thing that is similar to something, does not in fact mean it is the same thing, because they are indeed different. Is there more?

I made you believe anything. Just the mere minimum amount of information was needed, not even a full ounce of truth was needed to destroy you. A little piece of truth, just a fraction of a fraction, divided by itself is what I gave you. It was all I needed to persuade you to follow me, without following me. I beguiled you to make me your god and replace the King's whole order of Everlasting Life with Everlasting Death, which is the Second Death. The second death is tremendously worse than the literal first time you die. You know when I died; it was the day that I was kicked out of my very own home.

Agent O: When did you teach mankind to go to heaven as you stated earlier?

I made you believe you can reach the "Stars" above. It was because I know that the Gentiles marvel at the signs, planets and stars above. I knew exactly who to influence. I was in the Land of Ham, in which you now call "Africa" and while I walked, I saw a man. He was a young man; strong cheekbone structure, very shiny black skin, long kinky hair, big and fuzzy. I looked into his eyes, he was a Cushite.

Agent O: Cushite? Can you please clarify?

Excuse me, an Ethiopian; very handsome, muscular, well fed, and well kept. I searched his thoughts as he walked the desert to his sure death; his name was Nimrud. He walked in the deserts of Caanan in the scorching heat of death, destruction and the surety to be eaten by unclean birds. I watched him as he walked. I searched his mind and every thought, and I was able to find out a few details about him. I found out that he was in a war with others around him. The surrounding kingdoms of Erech, Accad, and Calneh all were located in the land of Shinar along with Babel. They all turned against his father who was of a ruling class of the Cushite kingdom and was Governor over Babel. The surrounding cities rulers killed both his father and mother without mercy. Even worse, His wife and son were taken in the seige, Semiramis and Tammuz.

Agent O: *Isn't Nimrod a fictional character?*

You Adamites believe anything you are told, whether it is said and retracted, or whether the retraction was said again and then afterwards retracted. Tammuz, Tammuz, I love that name. The only reason it is rumored that Nimrud was a fictional character is because the historians which I ordered to change the locations and confuse the understanding of history by changing the land and region of Cush to the byword Nubia to yet another byword bilad as-Sudan or simply Sudan, *and the icing on the cake; switching ancient* Abyssinia to Ethiopia in the 1940's. *I just used bywords to change the name of the people in that region. Fun fact many people on this earth are called by bywords instead of by nation of their fathers Shem, Ham and Japhet. To deceive you ignorant Adamites is so simple.*

Agent O: Is it okay to tell me about your Nimrod?

Nimrod was captured and instead of killing him, he was ousted and cast out to walk through the desert heat, which is a hard and long death process. Nimrod impressed me, he was a very strong Adamite who had the beauty of his ancestor the Eve, and the strength of Adam dwelled in him.

Agent O: What else impressed you about Nimrod besides his strength and beauty?

I need you to perceive that this man was cast into the desert and literally had walked approximately 200 miles in order to reach the area I usually just stroll through on occasions. Do the math; he was dehydrated and just walked along slowly in the scorching desert. At first I thought this was the most entertaining thing I have ever seen in all of my existence; well, maybe not all of my existence, but one of the most memorable ones none the least.

Agent O: This is very interesting, can you continue on about Nimrod?

I watched Nimrud continue on to drag his feet another quarter of a mile and I just watched him from the distance. Who am I to interfere with Melchizdek's work? I watched him fall down, and it was hilarious, I burst out into excruciating laughter, as soon as I saw the beginning of his slow motion fall. He is the first being I have ever seen this happen to. He also did something else I have never seen before, and he was a blessed one.

Agent O: What did he do that you have never seen?

I could not go near him, because the blessed ones were of a line of those faithful to the KING of Heavens above. I could not fully interfere so I merely observed as he fell to the ground to die. He could see me; and this too was something I had not seen since the Adam and his Eve, and their generations that were drowned in the Great Deluge.

Agent O: I bet you were quite surprised that he could actually see you?

This was quite amazing because no one can see me unless they truly despise the King of Heavens. He shouted directly to me, "Adversary help me, Ha'Shatan! Come to me now!" I quickly appeared as requested.

Agent O: Were you as stunning as you are now?

spite your sarcasm, I popped up directly in his face in rare form. I was coated in blinding light everywhere! I emitted enough light to shock one from death and back to life, but not giving you literal life. I just simply scared the blue hell out of him. I scared him so badly that the adrenalin produced, forced his heart to race to the extreme and then wah-lah, CPR.

Agent O: CPR?

Yes, he then wakes up from his near death experience and having no one else to thank but who else? Yours truly, most definitely not the King, because he thinks I did it and remember, he is weak minded because he thought the King had forsaken him, and he just as all of that time knew Melchizedek walked the earth often so there was no excuse for no man.

Agent O: In which manner did he display weakness?

He simply did not realize that he was a blessed one, even though he was told all of his life by his elders and tribe, he believed them. The fact is that he had absolutely no faith, and all he had to do was shout out to the King of Heavens approximately 200 miles before he started walking to his death. He would have been redeemed by his own faith in the Kings word, his Prince. The good legions would have been sent to defend his household, it was in the promise. But many of you puny, organic dying meat bags, do not realize that there is only thing that you need to know in your life, and that is the unseen kingdom.

Agent O: What is this unseen kingdom?

It is too difficult for you too understand right now, I will explain that complicated subject another time. How about you bookmark that topic and we will return to it soon as you finish hearing about my prized son Nimrud, if that is okay with you?

Agent O: It is okay. Please continue with your story, it is very intriguing.

Nimrud pledged allegiance to me for scaring him. Do you see how faithless you Adamites are? I simply saved Nimrud and I gave him power for his own vengeance. He fell completely out of the Grace of the King of Heavens because of his lack of faith. It was the King himself who said he would never forsake his little ones who follow his order and keep his commands. Man through all of these ages still does not realize that everything is for the Eternal Godhead. Upon his return to Earth, then, will he take back this possession of earthly things from me, and hide me for a period of time. Until that happens, I have a little permission to run around and tempt Adamites, but only if I ask for permission first. I seek the hearts of men, who are weak in the ways of the King of Heavens.

Agent O: How weak was Nimrod?

*Needless to say this Adamite was terribly weak: so I asked him, "Can I take you up?" "Of course he said yes. I know he knows who I am. This Adamite has known that I have been an enemy of mankind for a very long time, so I had begun to believe I was literally dreaming that this **Blessed one** is following me, so I carried him up, in a blink of an eye to the highest mountains and I showed him all of the kingdoms, including his very own. I told him that if he bowed to me I would give it all to him for inheritance to his sons' and wife. And I said to Nimrud, All this power I will give to you and*

the glory of all these nations of the world forever. I will give you
the glory of them: for that is delivered to me; and to whomsoever I
please to give it to, I give it. If you will worship me, all of this shall
be yours. The Adamite said yes. And he bowed down to me and it
was the first time I could ever get the male to bow down to me.

Agent O: Did it make you feel good, that he bowed down to you?

Yes, in fact it felt wonderful, because now I could get the
faith of the legion back on my side to buy more time.

Agent O: That makes sense from a standpoint of warfare. What did you mean by you were in rare form when you met Nimrod face to face?

I was in rare form, I spoke to the bastard Adamite with my
Lion's head, I spread my wings out wonderfully. I spread them so
perfectly that you could not tell that I had six individual wings;
it looked as if I had two gigantic wings. He then hastily made a
flag to represent me. A lion with wings, and a one world nation
to go under yours truly. I suggested things and I gave him earthly
riches to begin my mission to destroy each and every last Adamite.
Ruling over Nimrud helped me polish my skill of suggestions;
and to understand the lusts of men, and the mindsets of you flesh
bags. You are a complicated, simple, but complex creation. The
power of simple suggestion laced with bribery, is the formula it
takes to takes to steer you all from the goal to become eternal.

Agent O: I am getting some great notes today. So who would you say you are most afraid of?

I am afraid of The Prince of all things.

Agent O: Who is this Prince of all things? Furthermore, why are you afraid of him?

Millennia before man was created, there was an order given and immediately a meeting was called to discuss things concerning the space, time, location and also what will these places and times and planes shall be called. God exists in all areas of times, spaces, numbers, kingdoms, creations, and he controls them all, even through their free will. That is always the most amazing thing I have ever learned from the King. He gives us all free will, and what I mean by us all, is every creation that was ever created. I remember being in heaven above with my brethren. All things were perfect and in order. There was absolutely not one single thing that was out of order. The buildings of the city were in order and the Word was in charge of all the workings of the city.

Agent O: Sounds like things were great. How were the working relationships in this city?

The relationships we had was an unbreakable one and perfectly in sync, nothing was better than this existence. This was the ultimate kingdom to me and by my standards. I was the light bearer, I simply had the job of being the messenger angel to The King of Heavens, and I did a very fine job. My responsibility was to serve to all legions of angels, tons of brethren, trillions upon trillions of an innumerable number of all angels alike, an infinite sea of just us. I mean, the feeling of all that power! The way the brethren consulted and confided in me to give them understanding in the words of our King the Eternal, and his Prince of Kings, the one who is sent to do all of the King's bidding. He is a very dangerous individual and he only, perfectly does the King's bidding. He has no ability to ever betray, overthrow or disobey the will of the King. The King is his Father; our Father, the Father of all things, even space, time and nature. I am very afraid of the Prince of Salem; his mercy is not as the Mercy of our Father.

Agent O: I take it you were kind of rambling I sensed some uneasiness in your tone. Sounds like this son of the King of Heavens is not forgiving of any kind of discourse?

I am just very careful to watch my tongue when speaking about the King's Prince. It is a sharp two-edged sword one does not want to fall upon. The King is all forgiving by all means except when you willfully transgress His Covenant. It also angers him that people in the world commit pure blaspheme against the Prince and his holy messenger Jabril Gabriel. The Prince has absolutely no mercy on anyone or anything that is against the order of the King and his Holy Covenant. He only has mercy when he is ordered it be administered in certain situations.

Agent O: Can the sins of angels be forgiven? The fallen ones you speak of, can their sins be forgiven?

Of course not. The sins of angels cannot be forgiven because it is completely out of order.

Agent O: So, an all-forgiving God cannot forgive the sins of the angels he created?

This subject is totally out of your realm of comprehension. Stay in your place and remember that you are an Adamite, a flesh and blood being, organically created out of the soil and mud of this earth, pure clay. You are a being that is a creation just like I am, though I am made from perfect celestial materials that do not expire like all of the decaying organic creations that were made on this vile earth. Should he forgive anything out of his order? No, he should not at all, he is King and he is the center, organizer and creator of all things. Angels are celestials, created by the perfect hands of the perfect beings, in the order of the perfect and perpetual King.

Agent O: Are you able to explain to me why angels cannot be forgiven?

Angels know better, we have free will just as all of his creations. He is the creator of free will, but at the same time he has created an order for every living species known to existence. All of the animals he created has an order or a law imbedded in them. All Angels had the order of God sealed in all four heads at the first moment their eyes opened. It is what we are created for and it is what we live by. Those of us who go away from the perfect order all know and foreknew the consequences for any shred of misconduct. Since the beginning of angels all of us have known the order and his order for all of his holy angels. This is a punishment the legion nor I can run from nor contest. This is a grievance that burdens the entire Legion, which chose to protest the creation of the Adam.

Agent O peered at his watch and it was closing time for his session with the subject. He was quite baffled and amazed in the same instant. This person seems to be telling a history *before* the creation of mankind. Something that supersedes the Big Bang theory and the evolution theory of Darwinism he learned about in grade school, college and even in his professional life, yet never made sense, a fabrication of history. It was a very interesting dialogue being created by questions and a lot of things to think about because these were not the normal answers which indicates a person is having psychological issue. His answers were clear and straightforward, unlike missing gaps of information as normal patients. This man was telling an unknown history, in an order of events which seemed logical. Agent O made a few more notes as he listened to the last words of the session.

"This was a great session, sir, we are learning more and more each time we meet. I will see you tomorrow. Get some rest and we will continue at tomorrows session."

"Enjoy your evening Agent O, I will see you tomorrow."

..And the evening and the morning were the **Fourth day**.

Agent O: Yesterday, you made a comment that was very interesting to me. You mentioned the angels, that were created, had an order sealed in their minds at the moment they opened their eyes. Do you remember your own birth?

I remember when I was born. He simply called me forward from the nothing, from the same air you breathe. He called my name and I just walked toward him. It was The Word. He was the one who called me forward; and I saw only the hands of God, and two of the Cheribums my elder brethren, who have no name, yet serve eternally on either side of the Word.

Agent O: How long has "the Word" existed?

They have both always existed. Both have absolutely no beginning and no end. They are the epitome of true eternal existence. Their glory is so amazing; together they are brighter than 100 Trillion suns and more powerful than any sun or star created. If only your little brain could phantom the personas I am trying to describe to you.

Agent O: I see where you are going with this. I am following you, continue please do. What else do you remember?

I learned the rankings of the order of the angels very quickly. I was on the board of angels with the ancients of time and the ancients of the angels. The most amazing thing was that I was there when they created the laws for all beings and things. I remember so much, where do you want to start?

Agent O: I have a small thought. What do you mean by he called you, and you just began to exist? Could you give me more details about this person, the Word, the one you have mentioned numerous times in the past couple of days?

You want to know more about the Word? It is amazing to how difficult it is for Adamites to comprehend him or his position and role he plays in all of the creation. You have earned two PHD's and three doctorates in psychology. Born in Madison, Wisconsin in 1962, home schooled by two genius parents Joseph and Emma, and raised in a strong Christian family background. You had been reading the bible since you were three years old, was a junior member in your church home, and you participated in all kinds of activities concerning the church and community. You mean to tell me that you cannot comprehend what I am telling you?

Agent O was shocked by this personal and revealing information from a man who was literally homeless and just suffered a traumatic event: yet this man spilled his personal information as if he held the agents transcript in his hand.

Agent, do not be shocked, please let me continue: Graduated from Harvard at fifteen years of age, joined the military with an interest in extraordinary phenomenon's and special forces, became an officer, exited the military with an honorable discharge, excelled in your first job with the FBI at twenty years of age, and after leaving the FBI you entered the CIA and many other alphabet entities of government home and abroad. All of that grooming and education and doing so much, yet you are ignorant to who the Word is, Doctor. But my dear Thomas, do not worry I will keep it professional.

Agent O: How do you know so much about my background, about my life?

If you don't get it now you will never understand Adamite.
I have a serious problem with you, all of you.

Agent O: What problem do you have with me, and will you tell me how you know about my life?

You asked, who is the word? The Word is the one who has been
shunned on this earthly realm. He is exalted as the Son of the
King of Heavens; the creator of all things who was sent to Create
the heavens and the earth. He created all of the seen and the
unseen things of your world. You have no idea of the power of
the Word. He is the one you mock; the Prince, the Holy Seed, the
Holy one, the Heavenly Father of mankind, sent to do the work.
He is literally working this very day and moment as we speak.

Agent O: How is the Word the heavenly Father, when you said he was the Son of the King of Heaven?

Why did I call him the heavenly Father when he is the son of the
King of Heaven? Imbecilic, just as I expect from an Adamite, who
has a thought process that is rebellious to the order of the King. I will
explain it as I would to a seedling. The son is the Father of mankind,
the Father of Adam. He was the one who spoke Adam into existence,
as commanded by his Father, the King of Heavens. The King has no
interaction with any kind of flesh and blood beings or of any being
that is not a Celestial. The Word is the only one who was sanctioned
to deal with mankind, and only a few holy angels. We fallen angels
are defiled and now chosen for the eternal death or the second death.
It does not matter if we interact with you flesh bags of rotting meat
that is infested with worms and all kinds of parasites and disease.

Why would the King of Heavens subject himself to Father a creation which is disobedient? It just does not make sense, neither is it in order.

Agent O: How could you say humans are defiled when you too are chosen to die for disobedience? Do you not see that your statement is hypocritical to the things you are saying?

The Adamite defecates, urinates, and has to procreate to continue to live. Adamites are born to physically live forever, but has chosen death by way of disobedience. The same central theme Adamites live by for many generations is disobedience. The flesh bags cannot understand what salvation is, without a clue of what true Sacrifice is in this world or the worlds created. Of course I am a hypocrite, just as I have taught you to be.

Agent O: What are these worlds?

There is the celestial world or the invisible and there is the physical worlds that the Word created, and these are defined as planets and spiritual to you Ada-mites. We simply view them as worlds and you have let your own imaginations guide you to believe that these planets have life on them and that you all can go to the 'spiritual' world. It is hilarious to all celestials.

Agent O: How many Adams were created anywhere or any other time by the Word?

The Adam is the first ever of its kind of creation. The mold was broken after the first Adam was created. The Adam was the exact physical image of the King. The Adam was special because it was a gift to the King of Heavens and it showed his excellency and plan to move forward to create more of Adams who would become the heirs of the Kingdom.

Agent O: Explain the physical image of the King of Heavens?

*Just as the King; Adam had a single head, two eyes, two arms,
two hands, ten fingers, a torso, a waist, two legs, two feet and ten
toes just like the King has. Look in the mirror and around at your
peers, ninety-nine percent of Adamites have these same features.
The only difference between this prototype and the King is Adam
was literally a physical form, made from the dirt of this earth.
His skin tone was very close to the same complexion of the True
and living Godhead. We changed many facts. We are the fathers
of lies, and you love the legion. Adamites walk in the path which
the legion has paved for them; it's an easier path than doing what
the King has mandated; yet it leads to nowhere. The path of the
hypocrite is destruction. The same hypocrisy, in which I dwell in,
is the same hypocrisy we taught you, and you absolutely love it.*

Agent O: What skin tone is the King of Heavens and his Word? Since you have said Adam's complexion was very close to the Creator.

*Do you see how easily you paid more attention to the skin tone of
the creator instead of the history and facts I have expounded to you?
The one thing that baffles me is how it was too easy to suggest the
division of nations by translating skin tone into a thing we called
race. I literally love it because mankind for some odd has not figured
out they all come from the same blood of one man, Adam. What is
not understood or realized about skin color is the different nations
of people of the world, came directly from out of Adam. These
people were never concerned about what color their skin was it was
common to see lighter complexions or even no color or albinism,
which all came out of Adam the source. All people allotted themselves
to one rule, one law that the King put forth to the sons of men since
day one, and that same natural law goes on still this day, and that
law is, You are what your father is. It does not matter who is the*

woman males choose to have their children with, well these days it does not matter at all. It does not matter what your skin color is; whosoever the Father of the child, it is the nationality of that person. The Father merely ties the child to the land of Origin, the place where the man resides or is originally from. This is the same concept of why I call all of you Adamites. Do you comprehend?

Agent O: So each man no matter who he is, is the carrier of their generations going back to the land of their origin, by order of their forefathers. That is a pretty easy concept to comprehend. I think I understand, but we may have to revisit this later on. This is very interesting.

This is what the one called Enoch realized very early in the creation of man. This man understood better than anyone who existed in the ancient times. I personally did not know what the Word was doing with Enoch, even granting him the grace to be transformed into a celestial. I figured it was just a little humor. I thought, how could this simple image become what he is? With the Adam, it was an image, but when the Word pulled it out of the dirt it was glorious, a perfect organic being. I have never seen it done since then, it was so amazing. The Enoch was just the opposite, forming the celestial from the organic, which will be done again.

Agent O: What was so amazing about this event?

One of the most amazing things about this event was when the first breath of life taken from the Father put into the personal palms of the Word himself, who carried the breath of life and blew it into this images' nostrils, it was just enough, the perfect amount of air. This image, it woke up and it walked and talked and spoke. He called it Adam. It is so ironic that this very day, I am attached to the very thing I have hated since before its creation. I did not understand at first, but now have come to see that we both are just creations, I'm just better than you.

Agent O: We are having such a break through. What makes you better than any of the creations?

I'm better than you because I never had to wear that flawed suit of flesh. You are a fleshy soul and your soul dies. My soul is different from yours. My soul, as all celestials, is uniquely different; I live forever. I have no expiration date, but I do have a punishment coming for me. Only if I can bring at least two and a half billion humans with me this last millennia to the second death, It is not a problem if I suffer, because my mission to kill off as many Adamites as possible is not in vain if this is accomplished.

Agent O: If you have done so, how many people have you killed?

I have killed trillions of you in the ages of mankind. I create famines, not as the Word did in Mizraim, which was great work by the way; I could have never thought of that kind of destruction. I thought I was creative, but the Word. He is the most efficient perfectionist; eloquent, Great, faithful, fearless, Prince of Kings, genius of geniuses, the epitome of the King of Heavens himself. The Everlasting Power, Everlasting King, the Gods of all things.

Agent O: Trillions? That is a lot of people. Do you think God will be proud of you?

You flesh bags have no idea of who you mock, who you badger, and the most insane and illogical thing is, I gave all of this to you.

Agent O: What do you mean, you gave it to man?

I gave man suggestions and the promise of Power. You gave up being a God, a Son of God, to follow beautiful ole me into the lake of desolation. I love how you have twisted the stories of me over and over, rumors at most. Adamites absolutely love tall tales and lies that are pure fantasy.

Agent O: What rumors about you has someone created? Who has slandered your name and for what reasons?

The most amazing part about this whole thing is the slandering of my person. I too am cursed, the Word told Isaiah to scribe the fact that I will not be viewed as beautiful anymore, I would not be this glorious angel anymore, though I am the most beautiful angel ever created. Due to the prophecy as it was written; Adamites view me as a red tailed, bald headed, wingless, pitchfork tooting, ugly, defiled, diseased creep. Some just view me either as a jerk because of your fantasy stories. I look nothing as such.

Agent O: I see this greatly bothers you more than the fact of being burned forever in a lake of lava.

Oh, of course. Image is everything to me; I take great pride in my outer features. At first, I did not believe the rumors because I had a hold on many a men and I know exactly how to get their attention. See, we celestials can read your minds. The minds of Adamites runs on a dab of celestial energy so this is how we Fallen Angels can tune in to your negative desires and wants, which is about ninety-seven percent of the Adamite psyche, that thinks of sins constantly as defined by the Law of God, the other three percent is other simple things like emotions and feelings, and the needs.

Agent O: What types of Emotions and feelings are you speaking about?

Emotions such as pride, I absolutely love pride, I cannot figure out why, but I chime in on pride. Feelings, such a one like lust is very powerful. It is not really complicated because it is easy to show you how these two things; pride and lust is really both the same exact thing. You have to think about these actions in order to flow with them or agree to do them. I only come in to play when there is no turning back at your weakest point, which can also be your most powerful peak in life, I influence you to the fullest of your very own evil, to push you to make the conscious jump I made when I rebelled against the King of Heavens. I merely give them the tools they need to complete the task of evil but one has to literally make that decision themselves in order to do it. Many trillions, by their actions, have fallen into the same lake of fire with the fallen angels at the appointed time of the King of heavens.

Agent O: This is what you did to your son Nimrud? Did you push him over the edge into pure evil?

He chose the way, I on the other hand merely paved the path for him, yet and still I kept my promise to him for many generations.

Agent O: How? He is dead, you just told me that a day or so ago.

What do you mean how? The fur trees of the Winter solstice represent Nimrud eternally. The Word himself once said I see men as trees walking, and you will know the tree by the fruit it bears. This was one of the most ingenious quotes he has ever said in complete simplicity. He is always good at shooting zingers at you Adamites and it went over your heads as usual.

Agent O: You are speaking about analogy versus literal sense of things correct? What are some of those notions that concern you about the understanding of Adamites?

The problem with Adamites is the Word spoke in terms of eating, trees, doors, farming, vineyards and the familiar things the people of those ages did occupationally. Most of the Adamites of those ages has the same mentality as you Adamites, of this last age, not knowing that everything the word spoke is all literal, but in parables a type of ebonics for that particular age. The assumption of thinking to eat with your mouth to digest something of nourishment is ignorantly used when Adamites try to decipher the words of the Prince. Adamites think about eating literal fruit, or immediately when the word says food, eat or fruit, branch, vineyard, garden or tree, you immediately cannot understand that he is not always talking about indulging and digesting food. The carnal mindset of Adamites is the thought process he hates. This happens each and every time for most of the Adamites.

Agent O: Interesting, anymore thoughts on this?

If you simply think about what the word was saying, and read his scrolls that are scribed by his Prophets it is easy to identify the things he is telling all Adamites and everything he created. He is constantly speaking about what evils people will teach you through their vain imaginations.

Agent O: What kind of vain imaginations are you speaking about?

I will bring you back to the eternity of my son Nimrud. If you are well versed in the writings of Jeremiah, he has told you the exact words of the Prince. The word absolutely hates these traditions or vain imaginations, and he tells you that you transgress the words of the King of Heaven by your traditions. By simply listening to the word, he tells you every tree or person, which does not bear good fruit, or good works is hewn down or judged and cast into the fire or eternal damnation by the lake of fire. Jeremiah also scribes one of the greatest transgressions in the scrolls of the King of Heaven. He spoke about an event that happened before his time and that has been going on even up until this present day. He spoke about how Adamites would go into the forest during the winter solstice and will saw a tree to its demise and place it in their homes, and the tree stands upright on a homemade stand, though the people do not stand for the right or the good and follow another god. This was an old ancient Babylonian tradition, which represents the days of Nimrod my Prince, and his son Tammuz, the gods many love and cherish next to their very hearts. This is also why the scrolls tell you that the trees of the forest will even rejoice when the Word destroys this event across the world.

Agent O: Being that you hate Adamites, what made you fraternize with Nimrod? Why not let death overtake him?

I am the angel of death, the Devil, the Old Serpent, the Adversary of man. The word did not command any of the fallen, to touch Nimrod. I was in his area and given the command, I would have killed him in seconds. Since the King of Heavens has a son, I too adopted a son; he did the same exact things that happened to me. We have a lot of things in common. He was a blessed one, which fell from grace just as I did. Yes, I laughed at his would be demise in the sands of the desert, but he was the only loyal son I have ever had so I helped him create a tradition. That same tradition was designed to remind the generations of Adamites in the world of who my great servant and my only son is. The only way I could fulfill my promise to him, and keep him alive forever, was to create a new way of thinking for all Adamites.

Agent O: This is very interesting, so is the "winter solstice" the way to keep him alive forever?

It was one of the best ideas for destruction I have ever had. Man is an ever-learning being. If you feed it the right information, it keeps feeding for positive thoughts and positive learning, therefore adding the ways of the Word to the mindset of this being, it has the ability to be transformed to be a true son of the King of Heavens. I was the 3rd born of the Angels of God, first of the Cherubs. My brethren the two ancients have been around longer than I have. Everywhere the Word goes and has been, they have been there each step he takes, except the period of time when man was allowed to take him to the death. It was I who was first of the Cherubs! The most powerful angels, Adamites in their ignorance do not realize this.

Agent O: If you were the third angel created, how come the two ancient ones are not the most powerful?

They do not speak to anyone at all, they are silent always. I do not know how strong or powerful they truly are. Just know that no one, or no thing which offends the Word or approaches him without order and of course permission, will never get near him. If anything is out of his order, the ancients will not allow it near the Word nor will the Word allow any unclean thing near him.

Agent O: That is understood. How did you force mankind to follow the tradition of the Winter Solstice for Nimrod?

It was good for me that I was able to penetrate into the mindset of mankind, and seal the worship of my only son and I. I did it to the world, not by force, it was purely voluntary on the Adamites part. When you force something upon people they remember you and how you deceived them by force. They will ultimately rebel at the slightest moment of truth or freedom. When someone voluntarily

*does something it is a conscious decision for him or her to do as
you suggested, without forcing their hand, and they therefore feel
empowered as if this is their decision. All I simply did was use false
facts, which are lies and cover all of them with good cheer and
libations. You will have absolute control and eventually they will
run on autopilot and refuse to change or learn more. You now
have complete control as a handler. They will appoint their own
watchdog or Priest for their gods by showering gifts to the one who
continues in the tradition they have created. The Adamite Priest is
greater than an Adamite king because it was once a tradition for
the Priesthoods to communicate directly to the King of Heaven. But
after the Last of the Great Floods, Adamites in this future of Noah's
last generations; do not know that the true seed of the Priesthood
will be revealed in these last days and judgment of the first Adam.*

**Agent O: The whole idea of your rule is based off of greatly
fabricated lies and myths I see. Complex ruler ship by deception,
and setting up of your own type of priests to guide the masses in
the manner of your own wish. The creation of traditions that are
not of God, and the enforcement by people you have given power
and suggestions to?**

*Exactly, simple but complex, supply them with food or give them
riches and they will error each and every single time. This therefore,
buys me more time to rule over Adamites by gifts great and small.
I do not always give big gifts; I also give little gifts too. This is
only for my actions and suggestions to be similar to the King of
Heavens. Even some of the little gifts to the poor are from me.*

Agent O: How can you say that?

*Well, if you follow the people who I put into powerful positions
historically you will without a doubt see that they work on my
behalf and not for the King of Heavens. I have become good*

at buying myself a little time. The King of Heaven is always one million steps or more ahead of all things. The fallen and I must work extra hard in order to even scratch the surface of what the King and the Word have agreed upon.

Agent O: How are you able to keep up this pace of lies and deception for all of this time?

We must absolutely keep creating and evolving man's mindset through religion and philosophies, another thing we created called race, and false images of who Elohim is helps to create the ultimate infusion of falsehoods. We are the ones who created many images; perceptions, and we rule over Adamites by the entities of their own minds now. We suggested the creation of the gods they carved and created with their very own hands. Adamites absolutely have the power to change these things we created by suggestions, and to replace them with the truth of all things. Adamites could actually rule with each other in harmony this entire universe and beyond. But due to the Adamites having a very uniquely small mind, and its inability to follow instructions, it is pure blasphemy that this being is made in the image of the Kings of Heavens.

Agent O: So what could humans do this day, if you have misled them all of this time? Also, how is it blasphemy for humans to be made into the image of God, or what exactly is this blasphemous act?

If I were a human with the knowledge that I have acquired all of these millennia, to do the will of the King of Heavens would be my only pleasure. I know that once the time for flesh is up and all things come to pass, I would have a new body, a celestial body that never dies and is charged with the power given by the King of Heavens. I would truly be a god in his congregation of the MIGHTY GODS of the King of Heavens. If I had that chance as you still have today, I would do all that he commanded me to do, but I am not made in his image. In your case, you vile beings have defiled the image of the True and living God for too many ages. Your time is shorter by the moment, for the abomination of desolation shall show his face and you will not have a clue.

Agent O: How loyal was Nimrod to you?

I keep my son Nimrod in mind on the day I will resurrect him and rule the world once more having my son at my right hand to rule the first heaven, and subject all of you Adamites to my power one last time. I know that I will not be able to kill you all, but I will bring as many millions or billions with me as I can in the last rule, to die the second death with me! Nimrod was more faithful than any of the fallen, many of them despise me but only cooperate because they know the only way to buy time is to keep man falling away from Elohim with disobedience. We had to use our minds to think of how to deceive mankind. How could we make them believe the unseen was magic or craft, as a mystical thing that no man could understand? It was challenging at first, but the Adamites existence is nothing more than this simple thought. It is like taking a mirror and holding it next to your hand and viewing the two side by side. The hand is the physical and the mirror represents the Celestial, the form of the King of Heaven, and the Word. Do not view the physical hand as if it made the mirror, think about the reflection of the image you would see. Think about the image you see in the manner of its makeup, its components, and characteristics. The image Adamites will see from a carnal standpoint and say the mirror was made by the hand, but yet this is a case being made on the behalf of the form of the King of Heavens you are made after. The image you see has the same properties of the hand and it has five expenditures made up of four fingers and one thumb, each has a nail attached to it. Even if you want to go a bit further, joints, palm, but if you are a clever Adamite, you will see. The image or reflection represents the King and the Word, beings of pure light and energy not known to any other existence because there is no other existence; they are the epitome of all existence. They did not need to create a carnal plane, there was absolutely no need for the Adamite, and it was not needed for the Kingdom of Elohim to continue on for eternity. The carnal mind of the Adamites will think that the hand created the mirror or even the Godhead. This indeed is not true, this is another matter of why I hate mankind, and you are shallow and ignorant. You simply do not think for yourselves even being given the gift of free will. Out of all of the carnal creations of this Earth, he gave you Adamites free will, just as he gave all of us, all creations. I say he should have had a systematic program embedded into the Adamites as he did the bees, well let me retract my statement; bees are noble creatures. Bees have an order of all their works, and the Adamites are just chaotic in all of their works, just as some useless wasps.

Agent O: How does the Kingdom of God look? What is it like?

Even when the Word was in his form walking on the Earth, reserving his power that it may not kill men around him, the Adamites of that time did not believe the ones he sent to teach them his order. He presently sits back in the Kingdom of Eternity created by the King of Heavens, which has existed forever with He and the Word. There is absolutely nothing as beautiful as this Kingdom, which exists or has ever existed in the heavens or on this Earth. The feeling of peace you have just by being there as one; It over takes you and succumbs you. I do miss the pure solidarity, comfort and love entwined as one unit in perfect order. This is the feeling I do miss. And that is just upon entering one of the twelve gates. Untainted beauty and elegance with creativity unlike no other mind or power could ever conjure up in a trillion existences of life cycles. The amazement and genius is eternal and if you could count seventy-billion sunsets, you would have been amazed each and every day of your life. Adamites have given up the prize, the reward is to sit on the thrones of God in his congregation of Gods. These absurdly ignorant Adamites would rather die to become

*fictional images of angels floating around in the clouds playing harps
and smiling down on your loved ones as you are taught. The legion
and I still until this very day cannot believe you fell for this vain
interpretation. You gave up the Kingdom, which was already prepared
for you since before the day in which the Adam was created. I still
am baffled on why Adamites want to be angels, well I know why.*

Agent O: Do you mind telling me why?

*If you follow the big trail of world religion you will see the big mess I
made. Everyone is infatuated with the death culture I have created
on a worldwide scale. In this culture, I have created a mythical belief
that when one dies they inherit wings and a halo; I have done this
through many religions. It was out of my hands after I suggested a
few things and the Adamite did the rest for the purpose of the legion.
You imbecilics are only one step from your true eternal form, though
there are steps to this and striving to live forever by his words is the
only way. In this form you are the perfect good, all of your decisions
are righteous all of what you do is in cohesion with the God which
gave you the power to become gods. But instead, Adamites look at
fleshly and carnal material things as power and signs of good things.*

**Agent O: When can we see you? But, I do see you siting in
front of my face everyday in this room.**

*If only you could see me. Please do not worry time is moving swiftly
and it takes me about seven days to get this sword out, so bear with
me, and I will actually be fair. If you do not have me relocated
to a clear area I am literally going to kill each and every last one
of you where you stand I know about each of your lives because
I can use my mind which is more powerful than yours and I see
everything stored on that organic super computer called the brain.
I know something about each and every last person in this entire
facility. It is ironic that I am now briefly trapped in something*

I suggested a long time ago that has been very lucrative might I add. I am able to make man work for me instead of angels being subject to be ruled by you, which do not deserve to be called gods or even should have the chance to enter into the Eternal Godhead. It should be angels only! Strangely, for millennia, I could never figure out the need of the great hall we never used. Now I know.

That's all for the day sir, we have gathered a lot of information today. It was a lot of good information, uniquely good. Have a great night, we can talk about the ages of Adam tomorrow.

…And the evening and the morning were the **Fifth day.**

I had been thinking about the last thing you mentioned as we ended our session yesterday.

What was that?

What is your opinion about what age is mankind in this very day?

THE AGE OF LOT

I call this the age of lot for many reasons, one of the main reasons begins with Lot himself and the mere faith that this man had. He made a conscious choice to listen to God. He made a decision to move forward just on the mere thought of believing what was told to him came directly from God. He listened to and believed the details of fire and brimstone that was going to rain down from God, to destroy those cities named Sodom, Gomorrah, Admah, Zeboim, and part of Bela to spare his household.

Agent O: Lot also had a lot of faith. How intense was his faith?

He had great and impeccable faith; just to believe that he must literally look forward with his eyes, and to keep moving in the direction God wanted him to go is powerful. He did not forbear what was told to him, and to his family by two of my holy brethren.

Agent O: So there was no resistance and he just moved immediately, just because "two angels" told him God said to leave?

They all knew that if they reneged in any manner from the messengers of God, whom I hate by the way, that they would indeed be turned into a pillar of salt for disobedience. He moved swiftly and boldly with faith and yes Lot and his family started out with a total of six, but his two sons in laws perished. He and his wife, along his two beautiful daughters who were onyx as the Eve, began walking in the direction they were instructed. I began to rain down fire and brimstone on these cities, just as the Word instructed. I observed this was a very vast region of cities with great mountains, so the Word, as always was right on the call for fire and brimstone to come down in two ways. I suggested fire and brimstone by way of showers, yet the Word commanded me to use both volcanic eruptions, and to rain down fire and brimstone so that no one with a fast horse had a chance to escape. So I did exactly as he commanded and sent the fire and brimstone showering down from the clouds as the rain showers from above. I kindled four erupting volcanoes and began spilling lava everywhere, in every crevice and crack to hide them from the eyes of others for ages even up until this present time of information and technology. The destruction of them showed the Word of God to be true, and every man a liar. And even as the King commanded, destruction went forth and those cities of great evil, Sodom, Gomorrah, and all of the surrounding cities were destroyed in a blink of an eye. Man cannot phantom this kind of reasoning.

Agent O: Did you see this judgment as good; the complete and utter destruction of these cities and people?

Yes, the King of Heavens is all good, he controls it all, because he is the very reason all things exists, for his very own reason. He summons me and we follow his will even to the destruction of life that was created on this Earth. He is the commander of all and knows every single angle possible for his will to go forth even forever. Sodom and Gomorrah and that entire region of cities was very evil, they did things that we the legion of the fallen did not even influence or suggest. They were even out of control to a point that they even went beyond the things we thought of. All kinds of fleshly wickedness and lewdness was done in this region more than anywhere, and it all was willful disobedience on the Adamites part.

Agent O: The destruction of Sodom and Gomorrah was due to the homosexuality in the region, correct? Did the fallen legion teach these people that act?

Adamites are so shallow and ignorant to believe this was the only evil that went on in this area. How could a celestial being carnally lie with an Adamite and yet you think a celestial would literally lay with a woman or a man made of this vile and corruptible flesh you possess? All Adamites on this entire planet have a will, just as Sodom and Gomorrah, it was free will given to all. Adamites lust toward one another, they and their phallic and vaginal worship something I never suggested, but anything you do to kill each other I am perfectly fine with. The horrid sex acts Adamites do to each other sickens me, your thefts, killings of each other, enslavements of each other, oppression of your own human-kind, the same things also were happening in the region of Sodom and Gomorrah, there is nothing new under the sun. We Angels would have never done any of these things, if given the same opportunity as Adam. It has been too long we have suffered to see your species still exist, we hoped the King would repent and is so tired of your unclean acts that he orders my Legion to kill you all off completely and we would kill each and every carnal creation. But that will never happen because the King of Heavens exists eternally, therefore his carnal image has a chance to live forever. I hate the Adamites lies against the Legion and me, but I am the father of lies or suggestions I have made against the King of Heavens to his creations. They have lied and said we have lain down with women of this Earth, which is not true. Though we Angels are all males or the masculine, we do not have the ability to procreate as you, nor do we desire, because we live forever, and Adamites do not, this is why you must multiply, there is an innumerable number of the Angels so we do not need to procreate to multiply. He created seas of us many millennia ago.

Agent O: The sons of God did not marry the daughters of men, as the Bible says?

In your very own ignorance and hypocrisy you say you follow and understand the Word. But yet the word of the Scrolls if you have read them, tells you that there is more than one set of the sons of the King of Heaven. One set of Celestial sons who are the entire host of Holy Angels, and the carnal or fleshly Adamites. Both sets have a group of disgraced, disinherited, and fallen sons. The Celestial sons who fell from grace is I and the fallen Legion, and the carnal sons of Cain who fell from grace by their father Cain who murdered Able his brother without any of my suggestions. I hope you understand that, we all are sons of the King of Heavens and the Word because they created us all. The sons of God who laid with the daughters of Cain was the Children of Seth, the Blessed son after almost 100 years after Abele's murder. Those are the sons of God who procreated with the daughters of the man Cain, who the King of Heaven disinherited for the vile act of murder. Not any living angel has ever touched a human in this filthy sense.

Agent O: That actually makes sense.

It was written I would be a terror. I have lost my glorious form to the rumors of Adamites. I am now viewed as this terrible and evil being all because I know how evil this creation The King called Adam very much is. Look at how I am portrayed in this Earth. I have been portrayed as a carnal animal with breasts and a phallic, they call it a Baphomet some call it Pan and many other cultures of Adamites call it different other titles, it is so disgusting of the Adamite to do this to me. I have been slandered for so long and they chant the devil made me do it, Satan the devil. Even in this nonsense book called the Codex Gigas, they call it the Devil's Bible and they have a large false imagination of me on it. I have performed tons of deception, but I never once killed anyone on my own, I have given suggestions, or was commanded, but it is ultimately up to the individual to act on the things I have suggested. The evil of carnal lusts of all sorts comes from the imaginations of you Adamites. I was once Holy and separated from all evil, remember that.

Agent O: How do you feel about your accomplishments this very day? What things would you change?

*I thought I could disrupt his plans for the Kingdom of Heaven on this dying and desolate Earth. I failed in the Garden of Eden, I tried to destroy his creation and I failed tremendously because even with all of these billions of deaths since man existed, it still has not been a full Seven days for them that dwell above. For if you truly knew your purpose you would love your fellow man, so you may see the true kingdom. The True kingdom is coming in which a great majority of you Adamites, and the fallen legion and I will die the eternal death. The place designed by the Word. Which is why I will never see the true kingdom that is to come. The simplest thing I could teach you is **obedience** and you will live a wonderful life, I am the definition of **disobedience**, therefore I am the epitome of what being desolate is. I have failed since the beginning I failed my test, and we all have choices; even angels have had choices eternities before man was created.*

Agent O: When you say choices, do you mean free will?

Yes, Angels had choices, good or bad, wise or ignorant. When I made my choice I was the one to make the conscious decision to rebel it was I as the leader of the 1ˢᵗ legion of angels to lead the Cherubs, the most powerful of all angels! I made a choice, as so did my legion and we paid the price in our own ignorance. But in those choices we made, other legions of angels were informed of the true power and command of the King of Heavens, the all of all, the creator, the everlasting, through his sword, his Word, his Prince of kings, the everlasting Priest King, the son of the King, the one he sent, who will sit on the throne on Earth and rule forever.

Agent O: You said he would rule forever. But I know in the book of Revelations it says one thousand years is his rule somewhere in it?

For one thousand years he will rule, until the expiration of the flesh, the end time of all mankind, to usher in a new way of living where mankind does not exist. The entire Earth will be cleansed at the end of the one thousand year rule on this planet; all those born of flesh and blood will not exist in the carnal body. Your whole existence from day one was merely a test run for the eternal kingdom which the King of Heavens himself will take over all Kingship, and complete rule here on Earth after his son the Priest King, the Word, will be re-named as it is written in the holy scrolls. I wish I had a clue of what that new name is! With that name I could start a new movement before time is up! But there is absolutely no possibility that I could acquire that information from anywhere on Earth or in the heavens. Everything was already established in the book of Heavens from the very first day of all creations of Angels and Adam. He has told the story from the end to the beginning in each generation. I saw this blueprint for all ages in heaven above and I never thought for one minute that I would end up being the adversary or the devil. Sometimes things, that we perceive to be good is not always so.

Agent O: You made mention of the ages of the times, how many ages are there and how many of them have you seen?

I cannot explain to you the ages and times of the King of Heavens but however I can tell you all about the Adam. The time the King of Heavens exists is even too complex for me to understand, there is also a big void of ignorance that dwells in us angels, just as Adamites wonder about the origin of angels and even believing the fallacy of angels procreating with women, there is the same ignorance even angels possess. We too wonder the same things, where did the King of Heavens come from, who created them or made them King? Who is their father? But yet as learning through the Book of Heavens, we became knowledgeable of the works of the King of the Heavens and His son the Word who have always existed. There are absolutely no other creators, except these two, which dwell in the third heaven. But as far as the Adamite is concerned there is only three ages of the Adam. The first age was the prep works for the foundation of the creation of a being which would be the very image of the King of Heaven and His Prince the Word. In this foundation of things he needed something organic but similar to the very idea of the Celestial makeup. He chooses water, one of his most powerful creations. With this water he create the Heavens and called out the Earth from it, within all things is water or the presence of water, even the makeup of the Adamite is made of water. Even all of the planets, stars and suns, and atmospheres of each galaxy he stretched forth and the King and the Word are the only two who knows how far the galaxies reaches. It has been concluded as eternal, because there is no end to it as far as any angel knows; he is so simple, yet most complex, I have stressed this fact forever it seems. He even set the shores of the waters perfectly so that worldwide each shore is set for a certain point or tide. He soon created the ecosystem suitable for his creation the Adam to live in. It was the very first age, The Age of Creation. The creation age has many parameters but again, I will keep it simple for Adamites because of your great ignorance. The creation before man existed is no more than the time that was given to what you call dinosaurs and cavemen. These creatures were very large and used for the future purposes of the Adam, per se the Industrial revolution in the last days of Adam, in which you heavily used the remains of these creatures. They multiplied plentiful and they reached their peak of multiplication to the exact number the King of Heaven wanted. The Word spoke, and the animals by the trillions were covered under the crust of Earth, which was one large mass at this time. Centuries later their bones and flesh were in a phase to be liquefied by the Earth, then he called everything forth into existence to set up the complete ecosystem for the Adam and its generations. The Adam was commanded to replenish the Earth, and as the first phase of the Adam was completed only the seventh man after Noah was able to understand completely the purpose of the King of Heavens. The wisdom was passed down and was found to take root in Noah, who was chosen to replenish the Earth the second time, which began the Age of Information.

Agent O: I have a question about the caveman. What happened to the cavemen? How are we finding bones of these beings today?

Cavemen are poor Adamites which lived in caves. They were not apes. Everything on Earth has similar DNA only because all of these organic creations were designed of the clay and materials of this very Earth. The King of Heaven has different species of every kind of creation and man and ape are two different species and are not in the same lineage or family grouping. Adam was made in the image of the King of heavens and the only existence of life is in the Kingdom of Heaven that consists of eternal life with eternal beings, and of this Earth, which is carnal life with carnal beings. There is nothing else.

Interesting.

Agent O takes more notes dealing with aliens and other phenomenon that the man expressed his understanding about.

Agent O: Can you explain to me the second age of mankind?

The Age of Information

The second age of man is the Age of information it was written in the scrolls that knowledge would increase in the last days of the first Adam. Knowledge is the only power man has against any evil that may come his way, and it is written that knowledge will increase in the latter days. Has it not? Is it not written, "And many of them that

*sleep in the dust of the earth shall awake, some to everlasting life, and
some to shame and everlasting contempt. And they that be wise shall
shine as the brightness of the firmament; and they that turn many to
righteousness as the stars for ever and ever. But thou, O Daniel, shut
up the words, and seal the book, even to the time of the end: many
shall run to and fro, and* **knowledge shall be increased.** *Then
saith he unto me, See thou do it not: for I am thy fellowservant, and
of thy brethren the prophets, and of them which keep the sayings of
this book: worship God. And he saith unto me, Seal not the sayings
of the prophecy of this book: for the time is at hand.' Did not Daniel
the prophet write this? It is now the year 2024, It is so odd that even
in the age of information and technology that humans cannot see
that they all come from the same source, the first Adam. They would
rather kill each other to the brink of extinction, rather than to come
together under the order of the King of the Heavens as one body.*

**Agent O: Is the technology advances of today a reason why
the revelation will never happen on earth?**

*The prophecy stands and it will not turn, the Adamites are truly a
lost and very ignorant species. The age of information exists from all
things of the past. Every part of the world has a group of Adamites
who think they have done a new thing and discovered something that
has never been done before yet there is not anything new in which
they are doing. I find it hilarious that you all believe the Internet,
space travel, and your form of science and mathematics is a new thing
or something never done or thought of. You must remember that
nothing is new that is under the sun. Each generation has the same
great technological advances, but also in each generation of the first
Adam, the prophecy of the scrolls has ultimately played out perfectly as
it was spoken and was laid out over a period of seven thousand years
to unfold. We are at the very end of the Information Age according
to the scrolls just as it is written, word-by-word, historical events
over time, word of mouth, through all of the sons of Noah who now*

populate the earth, the first Adamites. *The information age is at its very end and soon the true understanding, in which the King of Heavens, by his word was able to deliver to a small and certain group of Adamites, his message and order to become the second Adam.*

Agent O: Would you mind sharing whom that small and certain group of people is?

You will know who they are and it is not who is expected. This remnant of people will tell you all about the Word and the destruction the King of Heavens has for disobedient Adamites. They will give you the oracles to the mysteries of the order of all things seen and unseen. They will display love as it is defined in the epistle of Saul to the Roman Empire, before their empire perverted the words of the Messenger in latter years and lead many astray. This remnant will help you understand what things you should and should not do; they will help you know what is sin and who is its father. They will teach you about the Friend of the Word, who taught from the tables of stone in which the finger of the Word himself wrote the ordinances for all Adamites to follow. You will know when you hear something different from what you are taught. I understand that you are an Atheist nowadays? But wait, you have been for ten years, even though you still read the scrolls? You will never understand until the King of Heavens calls out to you by mouths of the same people I am speaking of, the same people you have very strong dislike for. You will need to correct yourself unless you will be right alongside of the legion and me, into the same predicament we have. You will not become what he created you to be, yet you will surely be destroyed forever, with us the fallen Legion.

Agent O: How did you know that about me sir?

You still don't believe that a celestial can read your mind? Have you not paid any attention to all the things I have been telling you? You are just a simple Adamite. I am truly punished in this very moment. I have a sword impaling my body in which no one can see, and I am attached to a pathetic idiot, at the same time being interviewed by another, and in the same breath, I have to answer all questions in truth!

Agent O: What is the last age of mankind?

The God Age is the final age of the first Adam. There will be no more flesh and blood beings existing on this Earth.

Agent O: Do you mean that the technology has advanced to a point where everyone has downloaded their minds into a hard drive and there is no more pain and suffering?

I knew that even though you are an intelligent Adamite on the level of an Adamite, you are still very much ignorant, just as the rest of the populous. Nothing within your thought process has changed since my previous comments and conversations with you.

Agent O: I apologize for such an ignorant outburst, so when is the end of all flesh and blood?

The God age is brought on by the return of my son Nimrod. The same mindset, which was in my son Nimrod after generations of waiting, has arrived on this earth.

The prophecy of his placement is upon the earth, his power and might to command the ten armies that will place him near the center of the universe, next to the exact spot the King of Heavens desires to stand. He will call himself King of the Universe just as Nimrod, and he will be able to for the first time in mankinds existence call down from out of the sky the strange fire of the gods Moloch and Rephraim, which

*represents my power, the same fire that came down on the region of
Sodom and the crops of Job the servant of the King of Heavens.*

*He also, will command a statue that will walk and talk, this will
prove that I can give power to whom I am granted permission to
give on this earth. This shows how I was able to switch the seat
of Nimrod's power and mindset from the time of the Cushitic
peoples until the time of the Gentiles to show the power of my
spirit that will live though all people until the return of the
King. Since the day he followed me and from generation to
generation, he is the King of the universe, and I am his god.*

**Agent O: How will one know who is the servant of the New
Nimrod versus those who will not be his servant?**

*The mark of the beast is a sign of loyalty to the king of the Universe
and he will give alms to the people who follow him. Promise of
power with preloaded monies for joining him on a world wide
scale, still thus keeping his promise to Nimrod by taking care of all
those who follow Babylonia and her ancient occult traditions.*

**Agent O: I feel you aren't telling me something about the
God age, it seems as if you have deferred to the same familiar
topic dealing with Nimrod your son. What is it you aren't telling
me about the God age?**

*The God age is very complex but simple for even the most
ignorant Adamite to understand, if taught correctly. You
cannot enter the God age without knowledge, wisdom and
over all understanding. You will absolutely need to understand
what is going on around you or else you will cause your own
demise by ignorance, through the sights of your own eyes.*

The very things which you thought it did not exist, the things you thought were just made up and passed on to generations of men will all be revealed and you will peer on things that are far worse but more beautiful than any "space alien" you could dream up. You have never seen a Lion or any animal hold a full and in depth conversation with any human being. But this will happen. The world will be reset to liken the times from Adam to Noah when the animals and mankind worked together as brethren. Even the animals know the laws, commandments and statures of the King of Heavens. By his command they too were created by his Prince the Word. Even the pesky fly and all of the gnats, and mosquitoes, were all created by him and know the word of God and his Holy order. The bees and the tiny ants all follow his order of things and the works they must accomplish during their time on this earth. Even though these animals were not promised Salvation as mankind, they still fear and follow the order given to them by the King of Heavens. The King of Heavens is well pleased with the animals of the creation because they literally have done everything he commanded. Even when he took away their voices after the Final flood and turned them against man to require the blood of man, the mosquitoes who at one time did not bite mankind and which were great advisors and delivers of urgent yet private messages they were the ones you could count on.

Agent O: You are straying away from the topic again.

I am so sorry. The God age can be quickly summed up like this. This will be the time when mankind will be prepared to transition from a flesh and blood body into a celestial body.

Agent O: Interesting. Do you mind telling me more about this time? You said it would be terrible. Your answer did not sound terrible.

It will be terrible if you do not have knowledge of who the
Prince, the Word of God is. He is not your average celestial. You
have made the Word of God void by your traditions. If your
mindset is wrong by a fraction, or any offset that is contrary to
his Scrolls, you are ignited on fire forever to be eaten by eternal
flesh worms and also up to your necks in this lave-like lake of
fire, forever, but only after you are raised up after being dead for
one thousand years. When you wake up everyone you ever knew
is gone and there is a planet full of celestial beings that look like
Adamites, which look like the King of Heavens and his Prince.

It will be terrible to wake up to that, just as it will be
terrible that I and the Legion will have to wait and watch
it happen just as the Prophecy of the Scrolls say.

Agent O: What are some good things about the God age?

It will be the first generation of the Adam to have a chance to be
taught personally by the Word, the Prince. He will teach all of the
remaining Adamites how to enter into the God family.

Agent O: Will everyone on earth be killed off?

No, not everyone will be killed, only those who receive the mark of
the beast. He also will have perfect examples to show mankind what
they can become if they simply followed his commands, and these are
the ones who are raised up in the first resurrection into eternal life.
This is when the twelve Apostles will be raised, the return of King
David, to be appointed King of all nations and the Word the Prince
to be God of all of the earth to champion in Godhood to the world of
men, to be handed over as perfect vessels to the King of Heavens on the
eighth and final day. All of the Holy prophets from Moses to Malachi
will be raised as promised. Noah, Abraham, Isaac and Jacob, and
the righteous forefathers and mothers will be present. This is when

*the Saints of the King of Heavens descend upon this earth, once they
are all gathered together in the clouds of the second heaven, after
being resurrected from the dust of the earth. All of the Saints from all
generations going back to the first Adam himself to present times. This
will be a great gathering and not even the Space Forces of today can
phantom what is coming. I know you hear the signals and the bleeps
and blips, which seem to be a strange and foreign code of language
from another galaxy or planet. Oddly enough Adamites are ignorant,
it is not space aliens sending random blips it is the combination of
all the languages on the planet earth known and unknown, popular
and unpopular tongues of each human on this earth since the days of
Babel. The single blip translates to REPENT AND BE BAPTIZED.*

Agent O: How did you know about the blips?

*Still not convinced? Well, I'm going to be leaving here soon so you
may need to make provisions for me, lest I do it myself, and that is
something to think about. If I have to leave on my own power it
wont be nice. But your blips and bleeps is a warning in which the
King of Heavens has a certain angel in which he ordered to shout,
Repent and be baptized, since the time Adamites had found the
technology in which you use radio signals and satellites in these
last days, well, same satellites, radios, telescopes, customer service,
communications, astronauts, same things of Nimrod's Babel. So
now what you hear is the King's command to an angel which has
set up to shout this phrase throughout the last generation, until the
man of destruction is set up, then that angel will cease to shout.
Funny thing is that time is very near, and no one is changing.*

**Agent O: Ok, so its close, but what happens when 'he' is on
earth?**

*The Prince, the Word will purge out the rebels in both the camps
of his chosen people and in all nations that are upon the earth. He*

will purge all of those who defy his holy order and his hands, which
created the Adam. There will be many who will die because they
defy the very one which created them and has always had great
intentions for this first and most brilliant kind of creation. He will
now be upon the earth to finish the end of the work he started in
the Garden of Eden with the Adam up until the bringing forth of
the prophecies told of the desire of the King of Heavens to live on
earth. The Word will be on earth preparing the remaining peoples on
earth how to enter the final Kingdom to be turned over to the King
of Heavens. After each person is properly taught. The word will be
literally giving you a face to face, first class, A1 class that teaches you
how to become a celestial, how to become eternal. The problem is it
was right in front of your faces all of the time, but you did not care.

Agent O: They did not care about what?

Adamites do not care to become what it was created to be.
They are psychologically incompetent to even understand that
there is even another level to this thing they call life, but you
will never get it. Good day, I will now watch the wall.

Agent O checks his watch, closes his notebook and rises from
his seat. He nods his head respectfully and walks out of the room.
He goes into the control room and has a short meeting with the
Commanders and Senior Officers with high-level clearances and
other scientists and security personnel.

Skepticisms and wonder about who this man is, and how is he
alive and reading at nuclear levels and high radiation just as hot as
the sun yet the man is not dead nor is he burning up. The plans are
to keep the man there indefinitely, or in the amount of time it takes
to study this great phenomenon.

Agent O is stuck between science of things and what he has

actually read in the bible and has found out that all he has learned is a lie. The big issue is the Commanders and officers are not concerned about the conversation the man and Agent O has had for the last few days, they are more concerned on how can they use or harness this seemingly "super human" ability to survive or live with this energy or even use as a weapon on enemies. The Agent is trying to get the officers to see deeper than the nuclear, and to actually listen to what this man is saying because it is all biblically accurate and historically accurate, but they are not interested in the "prophetic and apocalyptic words" that have been laid before them in these meetings. "They simply say, every person is always saying when the end of the world is allegedly going to be since the beginning of time. And they would blow him off as getting "caught up in his work" and maybe needing a vacation after this is done and over with. Their goal is to figure out how to learn more about this man and how to harness this energy without destroying the entire earth from the volumes of energy pumping through this mans veins in a compact human body. They do not see the teachings even in this situation that this man is telling them they too could possess a body that does not die, but they will not take the steps to accomplish this goal and follow the wrong ways, instead of reading and researching what is being told to try and find the right way.

The Agent rises from his seat at the table. Agent O decides to just agree to do his job yet he has a new motive with his next interviews with the man. He heads out of the exit door across the large room.

Okay everyone, well I am just going to go home for the day and take a break. I have a long day ahead of me, so let me go to prepare for the next round and remember he said we only have a few days left to arrange his departure.

...And the evening and the morning were the **Sixth day.**

Agent O: What is hell then, are you not the King of hell?

*I take it you do not know what hell is? Hell is a condition,
it is not a physical place per says, but it is also two places
in one. I'm going to simply tell you what hell truly is.*

Agent O: I am real honored that you tell me.

*Hell is when you were born for greatness and a crowned
prince of the league of angels of the Most High God the King
of Heavens, and you are, what may I say? Exiled. I was exiled
for an idea of mine, for a suggestion, for an open mind. The
idea that I literally hate organic matter. I viewed humans as
organic matter, yes. I know how organic matter decays and
celestial matter does not because it cannot be destroyed. Sounds
familiar? I gave that to him; matter cannot be neither created
nor destroyed. Lavoisier, I laugh at that still to this day.*

Agent O: So, you gave the theory to Lavoisier. Ok.

*The flesh bags still can't get past that simplicity. So back to the place
called hell. After my views, I talked with my sector of the brethren...*

**Agent O: Why talk to them? I thought you were the leader?
You are just a foot soldier.**

*I was the First born of the Angels of God! It was I who was first of
the Cherubs! The most powerful angels do you not realize this? Your
home is not in the heaven above, it is the earth! The same place the
King of Heaven above desires to live! Right here on this damned
earth! Who wants to live here? Why would my great King want to*

live here? I want to go back home and I will rule above all the sons of god, and even god himself! I am the one who wants to go home!

Agent O: Ok, ok sir I am listening to you, I understand.

I figured out how to kill all of the sons of Adam, simply by making them follow me, in my ways and traditions. The prophet Isaiah told you about me but you didn't listen. You thought it was all a bunch of mumbo jumbo. When you bury your dead they are simply sleeping. But I taught you that they die and go to heaven. That's how I can kill mankind by words. You don't even listen to the Word, but yet say you love him. He told you it is the false words that men teach men to eat, this is what leads them to false doctrines and gives them information to teach lies and wicked indoctrinations of the imaginations of men.

People always ask, what is hell?

Hell. What's hell? Hell is going through your everyday life, not being sure of what you will eat, not knowing when you will get clothing, or shelter for just one day. But the hell I create is bigger than that, it is seeing these same people who are going through hell and not knowing how did they actually end up like this, yet you don't even realize that you too are going through hell, most people are just one missed payment from this same hell, this same consequence.

Yet every day these same people are not alone. The same working class people are competing with one another to avoid that level of hell. See most of you are bewildered by Dante's inferno, thinking and believing that I actually have a kingdom and that's good irony being that I gave the idea to him, more suggestions but the real hell and levels is the levels of how society is structured. Society is structured by way of Dante's inferno. Therefore society is Dante's inferno.

You have many levels of hell on earth. The homeless, the insane, the poor, the working class, the Elites, the Rite of Rephraim-Moloch, and then I am the god of them collectively. All six levels of society structures belong to me. The way this works is by showing I run the show of confusion. I do this by the Adamites who seek to be god-like but in a very bad way, these are the guys and gals I absolutely love.

Agent O: Why do you love them?

They are completely carnal minded and have no perception of the unseen, nor will they have an idea of what the unseen is, until all be revealed. Dante's inferno works in the sense of wealth and class. Any place designed like this is of my influence. It is the same as the kingdom of heaven I believe so, in my own special way, except I get to defile the very ones who are supposed to get the promise of Ibrahim to become eternals in the Kingdom of God. Well, then you have the Rite, which is a very discrete group of characters who are the very ones, which do all of the dealings for the Rephraim-Moloch class, and they do it well. There is no other humans on the face of the earth that can do evil more precisely than this very powerful group. They can touch you in almost any place on earth. But as I have shown them, it is better to roam for willing prey, so with power and influence, have they helped restructure all of society on a worldwide scale. This is to observe worship of me in some form or fashion. It does not matter where you are on this entire planet, I will either influence you or you will completely follow me to the bitter end. The rite is my soldier and they have made pledges to the fire that burneth forever! Then, the Elites keep the balance by keeping their foot on the necks of the working class, which do too worship me in ignorance, and they too are just as wicked and I feed them a load of nonsense they willingly follow. They all perform Child sacrifice and blood sacrifices and the voodoo non-sense we made up ages ago, just more fragments of worship of my son Nimrod. In turn, I keep them afloat with tons of trinkets and toys and lustful things. Since I am a celestial I can

*control the airwaves, another plus for me, this is my realm but only
for a temporary time. I only have a little time left but I am still trying
to kill off as many of you as possible. If only I could repent, if only.
The elites give the working class as what I tell them, and the working
class struggles to stay afloat in a smaller society, within a society, that
is ran by four groups, that makes up a super society which controls
them all. They pit the working class against the poor, the insane, and
the homeless and it is a perfect concoction for me. I buy myself time,
by causing confusion in each generation of man in every people across
the planet, from language to language. It was hard, but man has
been a willing accomplice to his own demise, by my very own hands
since the beginning. Even the simplest of cultures and tribes across any
region has experienced my powerful influence no matter how clothed
or unclothed they are, fluent in knowledge or ignorant to technology.
A lot of the histories they have, are that which I gave them. There
was always a way to influence the heads of many households of the
ancient times. Same as it is today, it is easy to make mans mind
think upon itself. Give it what it desires and it will follow you. The
society that I have helped sculpt is merely by influence. I gave the
good ideas on how to maintain power and wealth and they seemed
good for which it was petitioned for and not good for those who are
affected by its system. The poor, they work hard to try to get into the
ranks of the working class, while the working class is constantly trying
to get into the Elites position while it is slim to none that any will
achieve this, they can come close but can never achieve because of the
different ideas which are created for each class of people. Yet the poor
are constantly subjecting their humble beginnings, to jump into the
working class a force they may not be ready for if they are not used to
fast paced lives with the same process, home, work, school, repeated
in this process home, work, school, perpetually. The poor remain
where they are because they do not have the capacity to understand
that you do not have to purchase goods and useless items which will
not build wealth. I could also go more into the working class who is
my bread and butter of societies. They hold on to the faith given to*

them because man is designed to have a need to believe in something. They don't know that all they need to do is believe the word of the King of Heavens and they will be as he is in the resurrection of the dead to eternity. But man is so gullible, it is easy to manipulate him to believe whatever you want them to believe. Any idea or speculation that it will make him or her seems greatest among the people of their tribes or as the greatest on the entire earth. They will go without consulting the Great King, the god of gods. They will consult with me first, though their prayers be said in the name of whatsoever god they reverence, it be for me and not the god in which they are hoping the reverence is for. I was called the father of lies, and this is how I get my glory in the name of lies. The blasphemy I produce is the same blasphemy I use to make men fall away from the true King to worship a fallen prince of heaven, again me, I am selfish. I have no issue of them giving glory to whatever ideas it is they can wrap their minds around; as long as I get the credit and benefit of them falling away farther from the Glory of the King I will welcome this.

The Purpose for Mankind

Agent O: Can you please, from another angle explain the purpose for mankind, as you know?

Of course I can. The human is incapable of understanding their true purpose due to the strong effects of the mind vomit that has been fed to them for centuries. The human cannot see beyond the simple flesh covering it was given and it has not realized the potential of its initial creation. The first Adam was created to be just as the Elohim that created it in the exact image of the King of Heaven and His Prince Melkesedic, the Word. The men today which are the children of Adam which did survive the Great Destruction of this Earth by the Great Deluge when the Prince grew extremely tired of Man's constant disobedience to the King and the Word commanded the fallen to push up on all of the waters on and under

*the entire Earth to lift the waters as high as possible to flush the life
out of all things that lived on the lands of the Earth. Everything
died, all of the giants, the Nephlim, the mere failures of the first
Adams offspring. These idiots were literally the worst of all human
kind, super intelligent, super strong. Some stood as tall as some of
us angels, the only difference is they could not shape shift, all of the
Cherubs are able to do so, nor did they look like us, but they were
trying to figure it all out with their studies and philosophies.*

**Agent O: I thought the Nephlim was the children of the
fallen angels as the texts have said?**

*That is a statement made out of pure ignorance due to the fact that
it is written in the scrolls, that was given to man, and even written
in heaven above as a law for the creation, that every seed is after
its own kind. My good friend, mankind and angel kind are two
different species on so many levels, you would blow a fuse trying
to comprehend the complexity of a celestial body compared to your
downgraded Adam form of clay. The strength of the Adam was
distributed wrongly through a lot of vessels that could not handle
the knowledge, wisdom and understanding in the which Adam had
tried to pass along unscathed to the generations of his latter children,
the exact things the Word taught to him. The Prince of Heaven, The
Great IAM taught the First Adam all details of his purpose before he
was exiled from the Garden. He and the Eve were taught very well,
and even though it were all good that the Word taught to Adam,
though face to face, he was still corrupted, but by choice. What was
not calculated or realized is that for each move we the fallen made,
the King always is 7 quadrillions of steps ahead of you. There is not a
way, not a method to ever be ahead of the Ancients. Right before the
command of flooding the Earth, in which we had the great pleasure
of doing, I recall it was about 100 years before we performed the act
that we noticed one who was sent the Comforter, Gabriel, which
he taught the one of Adams lineage named Noe. For 100 years he*

*warned the people about their disobedience to the Kings commands,
statues and judgments. No one would hear him and amazingly no
one was saved except Noe and his house. Noe feared the King and
he taught his sons well and made sure they knew and understood
the words of the King of Heaven. I remember the flood as it was
yesterday. I remember all of the screams and gurgles of the drowning
Adamites, all brethren, the giants, the warriors, murderers, thieves,
rapists, a lot of the same evils that I saw in their ways, I see today. I
watched the generations of all kinds of people who stemmed from the
First Adam lose a chance to be with the King of Heaven due to pure
disobedience of simple things ordained by the King and executed by
His word the Prince of Kings. They just wiped the board and started
over and found the one he would pass his teachings to, and we had
no clue. We could have killed the entire creation if we would have
stopped that teaching passed to Nuwah. We were careless to think
we could stop the purpose of the King to go forth. We clearly dropped
the ball with Enoch who was changed and stored in the celestial
world to be preserved until the day he is revealed to the Earth again.
The Seventh man from the first Adam was the perfect example on
how to be a good student and Son of the King in the carnal flesh.
I still see him roaming everywhere on Earth, I have even seen him
just sitting in the center of active volcanoes and even at the sites
of great mudslides and other natural disasters, just talking and
observing as he has been doing for ages at a time. Enoch and Noe,
these two slipped through the cracks of our fingers and I think what
bothers us more than anything is the fact that even through all of
our efforts, we have not been able to fully ruin the creation of the
Adams. We thought that we could try to redeem ourselves worthy
to return to heaven above and take our place as rulers because the
King has grown weak and feeble. This is not the case, we totally have
failed ourselves and we fear him more than ever, and time is getting
shorter as each passing day gets shorter, losing daylight, losing time.*

Agent O: What do you mean by losing time and losing daylight?

You know exactly what I mean when I say this. Time is a ticking and it's a shame that the General did not believe you. Everything I am telling you is true. Tell the good General I know about this entire installation and each and every single person, animal, every seed of the soil, every insect in this entire area, I know its present, past, lust, dollar and desire, even its thoughts and weakness of everything that exists in itself and of this organization I even know the exact depth of this underground to air base is exactly 80 miles below the earths crusts and exits in four directions with a middle command corridor and the science center which is designed to absorb huge amounts of radiation and is the exact same place we stand. The good general and his associates think they sit safely behind 20 feet of steel and are observing us with cameras these last few days. Tell the General that before he passes his judgment on anyone else he should stop abusing his wife, he has been doing this for the last 28 years. But everyone else in the room should not feel any type of disdain towards the Good General, especially the rankings downward in the room, there should be no issue with Lt. Colonel Brigham and his every three day extramarital affair with Angelica Steinberg. Captain Bailey murdered Joseph Weinberg over pure jealously when they both were 16 years old in the military academy and his family protected him from persecution. Everyone in the room has skeletons in their closets even presently Lt. Jones is sexually abusing his own daughter and has enrolled her in counseling for a sin he has committed. Dr. Williams is selling secrets to your very nearest enemies just check the files in his upper right hand drawer of his desk marked with the letter "U" and see how many hundreds of millions of dollars he has been collecting for doing so. Still no better than killing someone, just as Dr. James is a habitual liar, Chaplin Adams is selling herself as a prostitute on various websites, yet who cares! I adore you all because you are sticking to the protocol; which Nimrod by the way of my eldest son Sin gave to you all. Do as thy will, Do as thy please and you accepted it. This is their darkest secret, hidden in the depths of their thoughts and mind in which no one knows except they themselves, and I truly love them for being such evil individuals, they understand the mission fully, and the fallen can win with minds like these or just extend our time. Even every man in this building has extreme dirt and evil they have performed outside of this organization. Except for you, you have been a fairly good individual, except some minor issues you can overcome with education on certain things you are doing wrong in the eyes of the King.

Why not air out my dirty laundry?
He commanded me to leave you alone, and to be nice to you after my laughter about your family's demise. So I will do so.

Agent O: Is there something special about me that The King of Heavens spared me from your antics of knowing the things you know?

No. There is absolutely nothing special about you. If I were commanded to destroy you, I would at the very second I was given permission.

Agent O: That's great to know.

You can also tell them I know they are not telling the White House until they have figured out what is going on. It is also funny that Rep. Jim Watterson suggested that this body be put into a rocket and blasted off into a crash course with the sun. It wouldn't put a scratch on me.

Agent O: Time must be short so can you tell me what is the end of man's time?

Man is only given up to 12,000 years to complete the last stage.

What is meant by this is there is an allotted a time slot for mankind a final existence. What you all have not realized is the simple things that are needed to be done in order to accomplish his goals for your kind, before he sends the Word to destroy this world as you know it, to correct the course and direction of sin we have caused by influencing you all with the suggestions and materials we provided. We tried to mimic the kingdom of heaven by the things we put into motion and to have things as close to the original as possible, in a reflection of the kingdom, but in contrast to all of what it stands for. We did this, again, only to try and subvert the order the King had already put in place so we could try to win our former places in the Kingdom of heaven. We even thought we could have more power and authority because the King had failed by creating this First Adam. It turned out to be flawed only in the sense that it listened to its mate which was the latter instead of the Word who was on the Earth to instruct the Adam in all ways and to answer any manner of questions which it had. We, knowing the Adam was given only a numerically calculated space of time to exist as a carnal being we began to work to destroy the goals of the King. As time advanced the Adam did not bring forth a righteous and understanding seed until the birth of Seth when he was 130 years old. In this event of the birth of Seth then things began to change. The humans born after the death of Able by the hands of Cain was not good people at all we did not have to do anything to influence the evil this human came up with. They were so wicked that even the most sinister plots and devices we had planned were not even needed because we thought the King of Heaven and the Word were done with this creation because all havoc was rampid through all the lands that man existed. These MEN were the Children of Cain, all of his sons and daughters, which multiplied very quickly in the world. They were Nephlim, the giants, nothing special about them just intelligent giants and these sons of Cain became tyrants even amongst each other, they warred and murdered and raped and pillaged amongst their own brethren. These are the sons of Men because of the action of murder by Cain who was disowned by The King of

*Heaven and the Word his Prince. Cain was disowned for many a
reason but one of the main things is he was disowned for is because
as being the first born of Adam, the Duplicate of the First Adam,
he was the blessed one because he was first born of the Creation of
carnal creatures which was to be translated into the Celestial family
of the King of Heaven. He failed tremendously, spoiled rotten, the
First Child of the Creation, the beloved infant that was supposed
to show forth the righteousness and Glory for all of the First Adam,
he was to carry the torch of what repentance is. This is the golden
child of the Adam. The first reproduction of its kind, the first literal
grandson of the King of Heavens and his actions failed him forever.*

*The offspring of the Adam, the heir of all things named by Adam,
given to him by the King of Heaven to pass on to his seed, his first-
born sons from generation to generation forever. The creation of
man proved a lot of things, but the main theme was that it was
possible and that it did work. The only problem that man has
is the misunderstanding that they can do these things themselves
also. Man has failed and even angels, a lower level Celestial, but
yet better than rotting flesh. But if you can imagine the anger,
frustration, disappointment, and feelings of betrayal the King of
Heaven would have felt from the one who was to inherit ALL
things he created for this Man who is to have the opportunity to
become ELOHIM? Do you not see? Imagine how you would feel?*

**Agent O: This is enough for today. You have made a whole
lot of accusations this day in particular.**

*Yes, take an early day today. Get some rest, go home
and go to the movies with your friend. She really
likes and you and is a perfect match for you.*

Agent O: Meg?

> *You already know who I am talking about, the only friend you have. No one likes you, except she does.*

Agent O: Have a good night sir.

You had better enjoy this night with me, my last day is tomorrow.

Agent O: Being that it is 1PM in the day, I better enjoy it then. Good day sir.

...Thus the heavens and the earth were finished, and all the host of them.

And on the **Seventh day** God ended his work which he had made; and he rested on the seventh day from all his work which he had made.

And God **Blessed the Seventh day**, and **sanctified** it: because that in it he had rested from all his work which God created and made.

*Someone is happy inside this morning, you finally kissed her, good. So what was so significant about **Keidra's Gourmet Beignet Shop**?*

Agent O: How in the hell do you know about these things?

I know many things, it is just that you were not listening with your mind. You do just like the majority of the Adamites in the Earth and only listen to things that benefit self and this is why man will fail if they do not do the will that the King of Heavens has put forth. If you would have really been listening to everything I expounded previously in the last six and a half days you should know that I have not been lying to you. I have told you the truth of all things you cared to know. Yet you rejected every simple burden of proof I have set forth for you to hear, but not of my will because I absolutely love to lie, I love to sin, it brings me pleasure to kill, hurt and destroy Adamites. The only reason you are getting the information I am giving you is because of Mikhael's damned sword that is attached to me, and if you do not escort me out of this installation by sundown, I will destroy everything in this entire site.

Agent O: We have a long day until sundown, so let's just begin to wrap up this whole experience we have had before you destroy this building.

So, any final questions for me? Because after this day is over you will not see me until my Prince takes his place.

Agent O: I am reading your transcript and I see you haven't been asleep these past six and a half days. Is there anything you would simply like to get off of your chest before you leave at sundown?

I know how this will go over your head, you will ask a question soon, but until then just listen.

Agent O: I will actually ask a question of you. Is it difficult or easy to enter into the Kingdom of Heaven that is coming down from above as you mentioned?

The Kingdom of Heaven is very easy to obtain, in fact it is so easy that it is impossible. What do I mean by this? Simply that the way the King of heaven and his son the Word decided to give their creations free will. Within the bounds of free will comes a very great responsibility. That responsibility is this; the King of Heaven put bounds and rules for all of his creations to follow. Every single organism everything that exists in his creation has laws and I am not speaking on the science of humans laws, no I am speaking of the King of Heavens laws for all of his creation. From the times, seasons, months, days years, seconds, moments, tragedies, accomplishments, all life and death moments, all of the seen and unseen is mastered and controlled by him. The word his prince, Melchezedek controls along with him and executes all interactions with the earthly creations, the King of heaven refuses to be amongst carnal creations. But the laws of the King are perfect and simple. His laws for each system of life he created has a structure that absolutely cannot be broken. The laws for the sea animals and life is coordinated to perfection, he knows which animals must be born to die to feed the other sea creatures to keep all of the species sustained for his purposes. He knows all of what is in nature, everything. He controls the earthquakes, the volcanoes, the hurricanes, even wildfires because he knows how much of the earth must be scorched to fulfill his prophecy that is written about the end of mankind. The problem comes when personal or personality is added to the equation of free will. It is true that each creation has a very unique personality and each personality is very complex from the emotions, to the very inner thoughts of that being. There are gazillions of angels and each individual angel has a name, a purpose, goals, and aspirations to be the best servant for eternity to the King our creator, just as every human born, has an individual personality, smile, thoughts, purposes, goals, accomplishments, failures, talents, mindsets, body shapes, sizes and hues. The list goes on and on, so the problem with free will is decisions. Are you willing to make the choices that the King of Heaven commanded and can you see the big picture and do you want to understand? Of course not. Man has always had a short attention span when it comes to commands from the Greatest Authority ever. The way to obtain the entry into the kingdom is simply by Obedience to his commandments, judgments, statues, and the Keeping of his feast days appointed in their seasons. Many have been duped into believing the opposite; it was a very clever move to deter plans but never stopping the plans of The King.

You are a being born into sin, and even if you just simply stopped today to simply think about all of the things you were given to learn, which are out of order according to the scrolls of ancient. No one is taking the time to teach the words of the King of Heaven. He has been sending a signal to man for ages. His words scribed in the scrolls are simple. Do not kill, no stealing, no adultery, no coveting, love your brethren, respect, honor and Love his Sabbath day of Rest, do not worship false gods nor images of these gods in the likeness of anything that exists because there is no way to describe him in no mans perspective. For the celestial have seen him, man has not because man has allowed his free will to go faulty and has continued to corrupt himself in things even the fallen cant imagine at times. Free will is a responsibility because even with this great freedom and not to be a drone ant that just operates a particular pattern, the possessor can abuse free will. It is very easy to go astray because one has the ability to make choices. This is where it gets complicated.

Agent O: Many scholars argue that the Bible contradicts itself, is allegorical and many religious leaders agree.

The word never contradicts itself, the word never has. It is man who contradicts what the word has said. The word is always going to go forth, it will be unscathed and unchanged. No matter which tongue it is written in, it will go forth and it will accomplish what it has intended to complete. The most powerful thing is the word. It truly sets bonds to the actions of mankind. Your word is your bond as they say. The very things you say and think will come back to haunt you just as the actions associated with the things you say and think. The way to truly cleanse you, is to repent or just change. Adamites hate repentance, because it requires giving up things that are evil and you depend on these things instead of trusting in the ways of the King of Heavens. The ways of the Adamites is just as the ways of the ones they call substance abusers they cannot let go of the evils in which they do within the laws of the lands they all reside in, through each corner of the entire earth.

What is an allegory? Is not it a story, poem, or picture that can be interpreted to reveal a hidden meaning, typically a moral or political one?

Agent O: Yes, that is the definition of an allegory.

The Bible is not at all allegorical. Adamites are just a slothful being when it comes to reading things concerning the King of Heavens. If you read the parables of the Word, you will see he always explains exactly what he means. If the explanation is given, no allegory exists because the situation was completely and simply defined by the Word. He has called people vineyards, sheep, waters, trees and many other comparisons he has used. When he told the disciples to eat my flesh and drink my blood, this was not a go for the act of communion in the churches of the world. I laughed to see all of the followers of the word simply walk away when he made this statement. It was quite funny because I knew what he was doing. He made this statement to separate the ones who were following him just because they ate a meal each day with him, they paid no mind of the knowledge of eternal life and even of his return in which he told them in detail and they still did not believe nor receive the wisdom to protect themselves. This saying went over the heads of the ones who only desired the food he provided and not the wisdom he spoke to them, he hit them in the area they most thought with, their bellies. Drink my blood and eat my flesh simply meant, keep my commandments. Peter knew the word had the Words of eternal life, which is the commandments. But the others who left were ignorant of what he simply was conveying to them, eat his words, listen to his words and follow in actions to show that you were preparing for his return and teaching your children the same. The ones who understood the were the ones who remained. If the explanation is given, no allegory exists because the situation was completely and simply defined by the Word.

Agent O: What was the purpose of the Word passing through Mary as you have mentioned beforehand?

The King assigned the Prince to create and take care of this world called earth, the prince looked all over the planet and could not find a single man that could complete the requirement to save the creation which I destroyed, I was happy that I thought I proved to him that this kind of creation cannot be and it must all in all be destroyed and never to be thought of again. I figured we could move on and maybe just do something different. But the King showed me something that none of us had even thought of. He found a young Judean named Mariam and she was 15 years old out of the house of Daweed (David) and this same young woman was chosen to birth the word into the flesh. And she was wed to a good man out of the house of David, Joseph and this man believed Gabriel just as Mariam believed Gabriel. The rest is history, the word came into the creation and literally walked in the flesh of the same thing he created. As he walked in the body that was prepared for 11,880,000 years, to prove to mankind how to walk in the very flesh he gave them from birth to death to eternal life as he already was. This is why the Prince is coming back to destroy. I am kind of upset about this because it should be me to destroy the disobedient. Not the word, I would love to get the chance to kill all of the wicked to do the one thing I have become an expert in, killing and death. The Mary was 15 and it's interesting how the numbers I had never thought of simply fall into place when it comes down to the entire metamorphosis of man from adult stage to the next stage. The age of Mariam fifteen and you add the numbers 1+5 and it equals 6. The word showed us the 7 at the death and resurrection of him from the dead. He became perfect. As I keep looking at the ages and stages of this creation I cant see why I didn't understand this from the very beginning when the blue print for the first Adam was directly in my face and even all the numbers was there. I think back to the seventh man Enoch, the purpose was not in my face yet the Legion nor I saw this coming. He

*could not be persuaded by any of us, he obeyed better than any of
the Adamites and after 300 years of existence he was transformed
or to help you understand, the word was commanded to make him
into another kind of being, one very much similar to what the Word
and the King of Heaven is. Enoch is alive and has the same chains
of darkness given to us by the Word, in the second age of mankind,
after the great flood. He is around he is somewhere on this plane, he
never saw death, the same thing that was meant for his predecessor
the Adam and his Eve, his perfect obedience earned him the Grace of
the true eternal gift of the Kingdom of heaven just on an Ordinary
7th day. I see him all the time and he kind of just laughs at me. I
absolutely hate it, but this is the will of the King, man will one day
all go through the Final metamorphosis of man to become that,
which is perfect in 8 days time. The numbers were right in my face.
I knew how old each person would be and even when he or she
would be born because I was the one who would be the messenger of
the King to all of these new beings. Lamech died at 777 years old.
The sevens were right in my face, then I even I didn't realize what
the seventh day was until I finally understood **the eight day**.*

Agent O: What is the 8th day?

*The Eight-day is when the Kingdom on Earth will be fully
reestablished under absolute perfect order and completed by the
Prince, the Word. At the very last day of his rule on earth after he
has finished preparing the last of the Adamites to live the eternal
lifestyle of the Elohim, the Final Kingdom from heaven above
descends with the King Himself and the Prince will then present
the Adamites to the King for the final Judgment. In this judgment,
this is when the Legion and I go forth into the Lake of Eternal
damnation along with the risen dead Adamites of all generations
of murder and chaos; the many I have lead to the lake in many
different ways. We all will step into this burning existence and be
transformed also. But the Good Adamites and Holy Angels will*

be the only ones permitted into the final kingdom on the last day, the eighth. The second this happens the Prince will get his rest by again taking his seat on the right hand of The King of Heavens on this Earth to rule for eternity. The eight-day is a glorious and dreadful day, but it all will be done in all the Earth, and the work will be finished by the Word as it is written in the scrolls.

Agent O: Does the idea and science of the big bang theory contain any accuracy?

Order vs. chaos, to order out of chaos

One thing people talk about out of ignorance is the big bang theory. They believe all of humanity and the entire thing of earth was formed by a chaotic and catastrophic instant when two large masses collided together in space somewhere. Another thing that is widely misunderstood by humans is this simplicity that concerns and determines where one will spend his everlasting. That one thing is order. Yes, this small but simple word rules all things and it determines all things that are not of it. Everything you can ever imagine was created out of order. The perfect order and way. See when humans think order they immediately think forceful authority or carnal laws. But order is more than you can ever imagine, order in a sense that all beings are equal in mindset and power, running as one. The total and complete body of one organism which then gains the power of the invisible, The gift. Order takes a lot of self-discipline; you have to be discipline to do as told for your own good.

Simple orders that keep you on the path of good things to come. Order can also have different parameters within itself to show you how powerful order is it can be split into three categories, which combine to strengthen it. Self-discipline, Honor and confusion.

Agent O: What is your version of Self-discipline, honor and confusion, being that you were exiled from the heaven above?

Self-discipline

A factor Adams forgets to consider is self-discipline. Self-discipline is just a matter of being in control of you. Knowing how to coordinate in the world of bad things and full of sin. The choices one makes is a test of your very own ability to make strong and good decisions. Every aspect of your life contributes to you being a good judge or a bad judge of the things of this life. Whether to set a cat on fire or not, whether to kill or not, steal or not, worship a clearly false god or follow an evil or brutish person in the paths of destruction and misery of others. Self-discipline helps guide one in the path of righteousness; by steering them clear of obstacles, which lead to bad choices. Adultery is a matter of self-discipline. It is easy to say no when one knows the consequences of disobedience to this order of the King.

Adultery is not only the physical act of a man and woman coming together carnally in secret affairs. It is also worship of the fallen angels who pose as gods that the Adamites have made tons of images and even new kinds of religious followings to these so called sacred gods, which is merely nothing more than wood and stone objects carved by the hands of those Adamites which crave to follow the wicked. Self-discipline is also the ability to reject the worship of these false deities.

Honor

Adamites do not know the true meaning of honor. They assume in their minds they follow the guidelines of what honor is. Honor is a privilege it is the highest mode of respect given to the King of heaven. This is what honor is. It is keeping in line with that high esteem and integrity, it is a tradition to be carried out forever. But Adamites have turned the honor to esteem each and every one of you should show unto each other. The order of the Legions of angels was and is still more in order than any of the workings or organizations of the Adams. We loved each other, we were brethren and we honored each legion. We were 3 different kinds of angels but all the same. Just as there were the three sons of Noah, Shem, Ham and Japheth. We were Cherubim, Serafin, and Terafin, but all the same. Our numbers are trillions of times larger than a human googolplex. But yet our order was perfect and we honored each other just as we wanted the same honor to be given to the honor and us and glory above all things was given to the King. The beginning of all, who has no beginning of days or end. We fallen see that we were right about the Adamites, honor is just a mere illusion to them. A vague and transparent form of butt kissing instead of what it truly is. A form of self-admiration and self-recognition for one to say look what I can do. This honor is false at most and is again a mere form of self-adoration and also used as a means to shame others who do not receive the same reward of honor. In most of these cases for honor the recipient is non deserving and it is always another person who is standing by as their honor is being given to someone that is undeserving of nothing less than death. The Adamite never stops amazing the legion of its inability to learn order.

Confusion

The confusion of the mindsets of people in the world is amazing. The average person thinks that the things in which they fight for are the right causes, they fight against oppression, depression, and opinions and the rights of things which cannot inherit the Kingdom of God on this Earth. I see animal rights being that which is more than the very humans in which God created in his very own image. People hate each other and it is very obvious that no kind of order is established in the 4 corners of this world.

The very thoughts of Men is wicked in all areas of the life cycles that are given to them. How could I say this? If you thoroughly examine the concepts in which man rules over each other you can easily dissect the levels of this confusion. The main thing man rules over each other with are on a religious basis. The religious basis is simply this, each and every region of the world has a particular dominating religion and each of those religions reflects the values of that land mass and the population of the people. The religion is usually based off of the ruler ship or ruling class of the people of the land, and the entire land is swamped in the mindset of the person or persons who are the ones who have the power and the currency to influence the way all things are conducted. If you have a Christian leader, the land will most likely be the majority of the leaders preference and also if you have a Muslim leader the majority of the country will be just as what the leader or hierarchy is. What these leaders do not realize is that each and every religion is the same exact construct just labeled with different gods or image of a god. These doctrines of these religions are very similar and have a hold on people because the thing that is in man is the fact that mankind needs to fulfill a need to follow some type of god or powerful entity which is to be the judge of their salvation and ultimately give them eternal life in the heaven above. Each of these religions give man the same message and that message is you can jack up all of your life and even be evil, but yet they are able to earn the gift of eternal life after their death. The gods that man has created all have a similar ending and that ending is the eternal life side by side with the creator of their particular religion or the false deity which is the only thing the people follow due to force and oppression and constant forcing down the throat of the people the falsehoods of each and every religion there is on this earth and many are met with death and threats when they go against the system of lies created for various reasons. The main reason is control and ruler ship over the very people of the land. The power is in the people to break away from these religious systems, but again the Adamite has the inability to learn order.

Man is constantly killing itself on a global scale day by day just as I planned and sin continues to grow so wildly that he has engulfed the entire plane of this Earth and there is hope for the legion that I can spare us a few more moments. But yet the King has already decreed that judgment stands on all of the Earth and all things in the Earth. All things seen and unseen will be judged at the appointed time. That is the time, in which I do not know, I wish I knew this time. Then I could know how much more chaos to bring upon this earth to make you Adamites near extinction levels to where you finally kill off yourselves to where none of you will be worthy to set foot into the Good land of the Kingdom. But you will sit face to face with the legion and me and burn within the Judgment of the King when he reigns on this earth eternally.

I have made you believe the Kingdom of heaven is but a dream. I have made you twist your very purpose to be an angel smiling and floating, playing harps in heaven, I have made masses believe the heavenly body procreates and has virgins awaiting you upon death, I have made you believe man will be given wings in the 3rd heaven, I have made you believe this.

Agent O: Do aliens or other entities exist as in other forms of life in the universe?

They are trying to run to outer space, build underground cities and bunkers to hide themselves, not understanding that DNA splicing is not creation, merely just tampering with something that was already given life granted by the King of heavens and The Word.

Agent O: There is no life on other planets?

You did not note when I told you Adam was the very first of its kind? Let me ask you a question. When was the last time you saw or talked with one of these "space alien" entities?

The interviewer clears his throat.

Agent O: So a lot of beliefs are just people's imagination?

Yes, whatsoever a man imagines he believes even if it is not in the order, way or creation of the King; man will imagine many things and we as the fallen give you the very imaginations you seek because of your mindset which is naturally disobedient to what is actually real. We the fallen have given you the space aliens and all of the fallacies of the stars of the sky and the sun, moon and its happenings. We love how everyone is dismayed at these things that are not even true or simply does not exist. We sometimes laugh at how man has built a machine that accelerates the particles in matter to recreate the "big-bang" that created life, all of the fallacies of parallel universes, time travel, the conspiracy theories of Antarctica and its secret alien manifestation bases. Adamites have totally lost their way just as in the days before the Great Flood, ignorance and rumors have trumped all things logical and simple to understand. Adamites have even gone to a new low point that they have conjured up the notion to explore space as popular television shows depict, this is purely ignorant because each individual will die from a hopeless and pointless mission traveling into the depths of the second heaven which has no end by the way, and simply die from ignorance and zeal of discovering something that does not exist. They too will be brought back to the earth and judged just as everyone who was ever born since Adams creation. All of these things I mentioned tie directly into confusion.

GOD'S TIME VERSUS MAN'S TIME

Man has the very ill idea that their time matters. Everyday its mili-seconds, tenths of seconds, seconds, minutes, hours, days, months, and years. The concept of containing time is one that man has delusional conceived. You can look at your watches, cellular phones, and clocks as periodically as you may, but that will never give you a true concept of what time actually is.

Agent O: What is God's time?

The time of Elohim and all celestials does not follow your aspect of time. Adamites tend to continually fail in each and every generation to grab the understanding that they are a creation and not a creator. The celestial Elohim the King of Heavens and his Prince who inhabit all times and all generations has even told you how to try to simply understand his course of what you believe to be is time.

Agent O: Where did he tell us anything about his time?

Today tomorrow forever, he had his scribes the Prophets write this and his Apostles in the scrolls of old and testimony for you simple Adamites. Celestial beings do not inhabit your time, you are allowed to dwell in his time, and he has given you a small simple space for you to see again, not even a mere fragment of a thought of His true concept of time. One hour with him to Adamites is three and one half years of your time. This in itself lets you know that he is far ahead of you and he occupies all time and spaces in between time. He is the forever. From the creation of the 1ˢᵗ Adam to Noah is 8,425 years and in that number of years no man has lived for one day in the time of the King of Heavens and his Prince the Word. Adam lived for nine hundred and thirty years and the only Adamite to get close to living in the flesh for one thousand years is Methuselah the son of Enoch. He only had thirty-one more years to go and he would have lived for one day.

Agent O: Enoch lived for more than 1,000 years, did he not?

Enoch never died, did you not pay attention when I mentioned him a few days ago? Enoch never lived one day in the time of the King of Heavens in his carnal body; he was changed and is not flesh and blood. The 7ᵗʰ Adamite is the example of what you all can become from disciple and obedience to the King of Heavens order. Enoch was a watchman and he had to be the hope, he was changed to show the evil generations of Noahs time that they could change, repent from evil, and to adhere to the Order. But of course no Adamites listened except Noah who was chosen to teach the hopeless generation. Even in the great flood, the time of God did not reset because as I have mentioned, he is the forever. Just remember that one-day with the King of heavens and his Prince the word is one thousand years. Man calculates his time by way of the calendar that gives you Adamites one year to equal three hundred and sixty-five days. If you think about it or even care to find out an estimate of how much time he has given you to exist is a simple addition move. One Adamite year in the Kingdom of heavens time is approximately three hundred and sixty-five thousand years. You can easily multiply this number by the number twelve which is his number in which he uses to divide all of the nations and land of the world, the days and nights, tribes and all things, then your total time to exist is only four-million, three hundred and eighty-thousand years. After this time is up, then new beings will exist amongst mankind and they will co-habitat the earth for the last and final one-thousand years of cleansing before the final form of all men on this planet is revealed.

Agent O: Sounds like we do not have a lot of time since the creation and death of Adam. I had better get to moving a little swifter with Meg.

I know this is totally off topic, but do you love her?

Agent O: Yes, according to the human definition and tradition of love. But what is love to you?

THE DEFINITION OF LOVE

What is love to me? The ignorance of mankind to truly understand or grasp the concept of Love is amazing to me. Everyone has the misconception that love is merely saying a few words or it's a feeling as it is supposed to be fluffy and peachy. But what mankind does not know is that Love is an ACTION. Yes, a pure Action that is at its peak leads to the fluffy feelings and the peaches and such. But Love is an Action by all means. The King of Heaven has always taught and expressed that Love is the strongest action in all of the creation because when you Love something or someone, you do, and you do well all the time, never-ending. Love is providing for the homeless, this is an action. You do not have to tell the world you did for them, you just do it. It has many parameters to it also, this simple action contained: humanity, justice, humility, honesty, long-suffering, leadership, servitude, all of the values one would need to be King. There was only one who walked in this skin to ever display it all. Love fails because no one is being taught that Love is an action. If you Love them you will provide for them and go above and beyond for that person to provide the safest and most comfortable environment for one. The love has waxed cold just as Melchizedek said. For if one loved someone they would never think to murder them or even take anything precious to them, there would be no room for cheating spouses and couples, there would never be spoken a word of deception. And this same love would be applied to all of your fellow men, no matter their color or culture or region. The King of Heaven explained that Love was the one Action that links all things with him. Love is the main ingredient in the obedience to him and his order of all things. If you Love him you do as he says according to all of his ordinances and objectives for his kingdom of eternity. In order to remain or be part of his Kingdom for eternity and to never die is to truly Love him and it is expected to be just as he has commanded and mandated in the Scrolls of heaven. Love was never meant to be wholly viewed as an emotion; it was more of a working verb. It can only be truly seen by action, by doing. One Loves his job he does the work, one does not love his job he quits and finds something he loves to do. It is ultimately very simplistic just as this, simple thought is. The absolute greatest and no equal to match is the display of love shown by the Prince of Heaven, Melchezedek the High priest, the I Am of all things created for the pleasure of the King of Heaven. The Prince lived in this vile flesh for 33.5 years (do math to equal God's time). He endured to the very end of his death to perform all things required of him. He even died on the roman death tool, the cross, all just to repeal what I helped the First Adam fall with, death. He figured out how to repeal death and how to save their creation dedicated to the King of Heaven. He loved his father so much; he went through the vessel Mariam chosen to be the Princess of the Promise the one to carry the holy seed. My brother delivered the message to her and all he speaks comes directly from the King. I myself didn't believe it could be done because we celestials, we do not procreate with the fleshly nor are we designed to procreate. We are designed to just exist; we need no seed to carry on our names. And that is the other reason we are so many, numbers upon numbers of us who exists. The love of many has waxed cold, because they do not know love is simply an action.

Agent O: So the problems man has is your doings? How could you even justify your anger at mankind, if the workings belong to you?

I am just more upset that you idiotic Adamites continue to follow me. But I am very pleased that you do.

Goodbye

*It's getting late outside, and my time draws near. This
sword is about to loose itself and return to Mikhael's sheath.
Once it is gone I will separate myself from this soul and
I will be free from him and he will be free of me.*

Agent O: I believe you. I will make arrangements for you to be
escorted to the proper area so you may leave. I have spoken with
General Vanderpool and we will be moving you to the designated
area by 7:15 PM so you will have time to get situated before your
departure from this area.

*Why thank you for your honesty and your intrigue to see if this could
be true. I promise not to disappoint you or our audience. Just tell them
they will not need the weapons, they will do no good or harm to me.*

Agent O: I will see you at 7:15PM

The interviewer gathers his notes and leaves the room. Meets up
shortly with General Vanderpool and his staff at their round table.

Agent O: General Vanderpool, Sir, he is ready to be escorted at
the time we agreed upon.

General Vanderpool: Sure thing, see all of you at the designated
area.

7:15 PM

Three taps are at the door and it opens from a badged security
door and the interviewer enters into the room.

Agent O: Are you ready to go?

Yes, I am ready.

The man stands up and walks out of the room he has been held in for six days straight without any contact with the outside world. He looks behind him at the reminder that he was held against his will by an unknown organization and is in awe at what has happened to him and at the same time he is in a state of realization that no one would ever believe his story. He is trapped in his own body that was taken over for six days and in this case it was not illicit or experimental drugs he ingested. This case is something that will not be know unless he did something to make it known, but yet he is compelled to be humble and not say a word, not only because this entity has taken over and not allowed him to speak, but from the sheer humbled way of thinking that now overwhelmed him. He decided to just sit back and not fight the outcome of this situation even to death because it was a power that he could not fight. He still could not speak or control his own body, yet he knew he was still alive, he still existed and this thing that possessed his body knew his entire life story. Yet he was now allowed to see out of his own eyes at the same time the energy of this entity controlled his each and every move and there was nothing he cold do. For six days he had to hear how wrong mankind was, the gruesome history of mankind and its fall from its true purpose, the historical players who all changed the course of time and all religions by simply submitting to an angel and his words of falsehood laced with good tidings, decorations, and wild extravagant parties disguised as religious events. The deception filled his mind and angered him to a point if he could have an outburst he would but he could not for he was not in control. He walked along with the interviewer down the long hall to a vehicle that was for tunnel traveling, something he had never seen before, and entered the transport with the interviewer. They quickly zoomed off and arrived at the location that was agreed upon.

They exited the zoom pod thingy and stepped on to an elevator, which is about 20ft wide, and they are quiet as they go up and they begin to travel up towards the surface.

The alien speaks to the man whose body he was attached to and it is quite surprising to the man because the entire time the alien did not allow him to speak for a period of almost seven complete days.

I am not going to allow you to speak, but you can think. You will listen and do exactly what I say if you want to live. You will be killed if you do not listen to me and do as I instruct. Do you understand?

Yes, I understand everything you have said these
last days of my life which I cannot count buts
seems to feel like three years have gone by.

Firstly, I absolutely do not care. I am only obligated to tell you this one last truth before this sword goes home to Mikhael. I literally do not care if you live or die.

I am listening.

They are going to kill you, pass out when I exit your body. Fall down to the ground and do not move. I will see you all soon at the finale.

As they walk out of the cavern which disguised the interviewer is silent as they begin to walk out towards the open area that leads towards a high-tech launch area with an airstrip that no base on the earth has. They get onto a cart and is escorted out to an area where everyone was clothed with hazmat suits like a scene from E.T. and other space alien movies. The sun was going down as 7:30PM approached and the sun began to sink in the background filled with the beautiful hues of colors and patterns of sunlight and clouds, a truly breathtaking moment.

THE APPEARING OF SATAN AND THE LEGION

*18 And he said unto them, I beheld Satan
as lightning fall from heaven.*

*In about five minutes it will be 7:30 and the sun will be down.
Things will happen that will most definitely scare someone
to death because everyone is not ready to see who we are.*

Agent O: We?

The timer struck at 7:30 and the sun was down in the horizon and lightning began to pour from all directions and the entire sky was filled with flashes that zapped everywhere on the grounds of this great facility. The lightning poured to the ground as buckets of water and it continued heavily as if it were not going to stop. Many of the men who were in the area to escort the man to the center of the field were consumed by the heavy voltage from the lightning. The Interviewer was startled by the tremendous event as the silent alarms sounded to alert the soldiers on the facility to make ready for any thing. The man walked away from the Interviewer and held his arms towards the sky and what seems as a golden glow of light that came from the most eastern direction but yet this beam was coming directly from above as if shot past the moon and the stars directly upward and it grew more brighter as it began to pierce the back of the man. A giant Golden sword began to withdraw from the man's back in what seemed to be a painless process because he did not scream or flinch from the sword that was greatly disproportionate from his body. The sword measured approximately 25 inches in width having an 8-foot blade and a 4-foot handle made of what looks like gold and an Ivory handle. The sword drew out with great care as not to hurt the man and then after it was safely out of the man's flesh, it darted out violently through the path of golden light that beamed past what looked like another layer of existence beyond what our naked eyes can actually see. Suddenly another beam of light came from the man but in the front side of his body and a large hoof of what seemed as a cows foot but much larger steps of out the man as if one was taking off a pair of pajamas, yet not harming the man at all in the process. The being stood erect and is a stunning 12 feet tall and has a wingspan of 24 feet.

The power of this creature caused everyone on the entire base to fall down to their knees in which felt like a aftershock after demolitions blasts magnified times 10, but not killing anyone who was not already marked for death.

The blast was felt for the entire 50 mile radius of the secret base and many had heart attacks in the facility and the majority of those victims were the ones who were able to lay their eyes upon the last being they would see before the last day. This being was a burned black color, which shined brightly and yet it was so beautiful and flawlessly perfect in beautiful by all standards. But the most ferocious feature about this creature is that it possessed four heads that was attached to this one body, which stood erect and walked as a man would walk, which made it appear as a man, yet was something else. He sparkled like burnished brass and all four faces spoke at once when it engaged in a conversation. The main face it used was the face on the left hand side of the giant bullock or oxen looking bull creature that had horns like a long horn bull, but with the other faces on the right hand side the face of a lion, and a man, he did not use them to the extent of the horned beast face. He was encrusted in all kinds of precious and rare stones but the main ones stood out such as the diamonds that melted across his body as a glaze from a finely polished doughnut that is then dipped in fine jewelry such as the Sardis, topaz, and the diamond, the beryl, the onyx, and the jasper, the sapphire, the emerald, and the carbuncle, and gold that seemed to be laced to his person in layers and a beautiful garment covered him made from a material not found on this planet.

The Fallen Legion appears

Just as soon as you get to focus on the appearance of this extraordinary being who appears out of the man's body, the lightning storm is still happening on this base and out of the lightning the same kind of beings step forward out of the lightning and the all have four faces just as the being who is covered with all of the precious stones as a sort of indicator he was indeed the leader as he had told the interviewer. The man fell down to the ground and ask God for forgiveness, being that in his heart he had resentment for God because of the death of his loved ones years ago and he pretended to pass out, but closed his eyes in fear of the ferocious and terrible yet beautiful beings appeared. It was about 600 of these types of beings who walked out of the lightning and one walked up to this being and stood at his left hand side. These beings had the same great wings with that dreadful wingspan, but as the interviewer as scared as he was also, was able to see the eyes which covered the wings of all of these creatures which blinked and seemed to be functioning eyes, though they covered the wings of these creatures on the front side and the rear of it giving these creatures a full view around their entire body and they could see in all directions. All of the creatures had a sheaf with a tremendous sword in it but not anything as stunning and beautiful as the sword that removed itself from the man and then zoomed off through the golden light, darting off into the upper heavens. These creatures seemed to be in order with each other and the Alien who was the leader stood as the man's body lay there as if he were sleep or dead, yet he was praying in his mind that he live through this due to the new information he received from the alien as he was abducted and trapped inside his own body.

The alien used the face of the eagle to his far left to speak with the alien which walked up to stand by his side at the same time the lightning storm ceased and smoke arose in zigzag patterns from the earth that was hit by this phenomenal storm. The ground was fried from the great amounts of energy from the lightning.

Alien: Prince Azazel, are the brigades prepared?

Azazel: Yes, Prince Ha'Shatan all 6 brigades of the entire legion are prepared.

Prince Ha'Shatan: This is the final assault on the Adamites; it is time for even more lies and deception because Prince Mikhael has held me up for seven days with his antics. Yet we don't have much time to destroy the beings of this Earth. Dispatch them immediately!

Azazel: Indeed. I will lead the attack in the western hemisphere; there are certain countries and Adamites to influence to do more evil to each other.

Prince Ha'Shatan: I have a meeting that is soon coming; it is almost time to introduce my re-born son Nimrod to the world. I will meet you at the designated area in a day.

The fallen prince turns around and addresses the Legion.

Prince Ha'Shatan: Dispatch to your posts to lead the rest of the legion!

The Leaders of the legion all take off in different directions leaving in a blast of energy and disappearing into thin air. Prince Ha'Shatan turns to the interviewer, and looks at him with his main face, which is the Bulls head with the Great horns spanning seven feet. This massive and terrible creature of high intelligence pierced the very mind of the interviewer.

Prince Ha'Shatan: Thomas, you have nothing to say about me? I thought we built a type of relationship these last seven days? I told you literally everything about me, yet you look at me with distrust?

Thomas stared nervously, but he dug down deep inside of himself and even tried to stand up on his own feet but he could not. But he was able to conjure up some strength to speak his last question to Prince Ha'Shatan before this moment was over.

Thomas: Why does the whole world have to suffer because of Adam and Eve's faults? Why were they not discarded and the King of heaven begins over?

Prince Ha'Shatan: Is there a King you know of that starts over? How can the Kings of the earth never take back or start over traditions or ordinances and mandates they or their predecessors in any kingdom of the earth? It is merely spit in the face of the King of Heavens to want him to recreate something he created to have free will to follow his order. It is the same reason we angels of the fallen legion cannot be forgiven and start over. We fell out of his order, so we must suffer, just as the Adamites who fall out of his order or do not want to follow his Kingdom and order will have the same fate of the fallen legion. There are no do overs for pure evil. Even after I have told you the truth of things and even revealed myself to you and my evils and transgressions, you will still gather in honor of me and Nimrod my son and disciple on December 25th, see even in this situation I did my job for this short period of time but yet you Adamites will continue to do the things I set forth to your very own destruction, this is how I win each time even in a losing effort. I already know I will burn for the things I have done, the comedic relief to me is that Adamites think they cannot suffer this same fate. Keep being disobedient; keep up the destruction I taught you, Simpletons.

Prince Ha'Shatan turns and fly's away slowly at first then bursts into light speed towards the most eastern direction, headed to another country in another hemisphere.

Thomas looked around and saw all of the dead who were killed by the lightning storm. He went over to Jude, who was now finally free of his demon. The adversary all men feared presented himself and his soldiers as no one ever expected and left his mark of death and deception around him. Thomas quickly called for backup and checked the man for a pulse and paramedics of the base quickly rushed to the area to assist those in need and to take away the dead.

Thomas saw a piece of parched scroll that lay on the ground where the sword was removed from the man's body and it was located not far from where he was laying. He picked up the paper and looked at it in amazement, he then folded up the piece of paper and put it in the front right hand pocket of his jeans. The emergency response teams arrived and began to secure the dead and the injured personnel and the HAZMAT and Fire Prevention teams moved into position to clear up debris and anything that could possibly be radioactive or on fire.

Thomas walked towards the recovery vehicle and got in, he was quickly attended to and examined by the HAZMAT team members for radiation and there was no trace of it anywhere. It was just as the extreme levels of energy that could have destroyed the entire earth simply dissipated in an instant into thin air. The realization of what just transpired these last seven days seemed to have Thomas in a dream state as if he had just been drifting in a reality that did not exist. A reality that was developed by many different forms of indoctrination by religious views of mankind, the many cover-ups and lies depicted to be true all settled in his head as he thought on the many things that are and aren't, things and ideas that are concrete and superficial.

The evidence and facts presented did make it truly seem as if the world we live in only exists of three simple layers Prince Ha'Shatan spoke about; the three heavens which is Earth, the first, the area or space between earth and the second heaven is merely separated by leaping into the air, consisting of the sun, moon, stars and all planets and all rotate around the earth, the space we have traveled and sent space probes and drones, this is all the second heaven and the third heaven is that space we have been observing for decades, that space we could never figure out, and we always wondered what this body of water could be which stretches over all of the galaxies and there is nothing that we could actually come up with and there was no explanation, man has continued to explore all other parts of the galaxies and universes. In the same instances man has accomplished great feats by space exploration by powerful telescopes and observatories, man has created fallacies as time went on, teaching things that are not true, leaning on their own understanding of the biggest to littlest life forms on this planet. Thomas grew weary in his mind, but he remained optimistic, because he now understood more than he ever knew about the unknown God.

Jude: Where do we go from here?

Thomas: We heard it all out of the horse's mouth, yet we could start over from here.

Thomas pulls out the small parchment paper out of his front pocket and looked at it briefly, and he handed it to the man.

*...on the **eighth day** you shall give it to Me.*

The Second Death

The Lord shall be known toward his servants, and his indignation toward his enemies, I saw an angel come down from heaven, having the key of the bottomless pit and a great chain in his hand, And he laid hold on the dragon, that old serpent, which is the Devil, and Satan, and bound him a thousand years, And cast him into the bottomless pit, and shut him up, and set a seal upon him, that he should deceive the nations no more, till the thousand years should be fulfilled: and after that he must be loosed a little season, And I saw thrones, and they sat upon them, and judgment was given unto them: and I saw the souls of them that were beheaded for the witness of Jesus, and for the word of God, and which had not worshipped the beast, neither his image, neither had received his mark upon their foreheads, or in their hands; and they lived and reigned with Christ a thousand years. But the rest of the dead lived not again until the thousand years were finished. This is the first resurrection. Blessed and holy is he that hath part in the first resurrection: on such the second death hath no power, but they shall be priests of God and of Christ, and shall reign with him a thousand years, in the last days it shall come to pass, that the mountain of the house of the Lord shall be established in the top of the mountains, and it shall be exalted above the hills; and people shall flow unto it. And many nations shall come, and say, Come, and let us go up to the mountain of the Lord, and to the house of the God of Jacob; and he will teach us of his ways, and we will walk in his paths: for the law shall go forth of Zion, and the word of the Lord from Jerusalem.

He read from the book of the law of God daily, from the first day to the last day And they celebrated the feast seven days, and on the eighth day there was a solemn assembly according to the ordinance. And he shall judge among many people, and rebuke strong nations afar off; and they shall beat their swords into plowshares, and their spears into pruninghooks: nation shall not lift up a sword against nation, neither shall they learn war any more. But they shall sit every man under his vine and under his fig tree; and none shall make them afraid: for the mouth of the Lord of hosts hath spoken it. For all people will walk every one in the name of his god, and we will walk in the name of the Lord our God for ever and ever. I heard a great voice out of heaven saying,

Behold, the tabernacle of God is with men, and he will dwell with them, and they shall be his people, and God himself shall be with them, and be their God. He that overcometh shall inherit all things; and I will be his God, and he shall be my son. But the fearful, and unbelieving, and the abominable, and murderers, and whoremongers, and sorcerers, and idolaters, and all liars, shall have their part in the lake which burneth with fire and brimstone: which is the second death. For, behold, the Lord will come with fire, and with his chariots like a whirlwind, to render his anger with fury, and his rebuke with flames of fire. For by fire and by his sword will the Lord plead with all flesh: and the slain of the Lord shall be many. They that sanctify themselves, and purify themselves in the gardens behind one tree in the midst, eating swine's flesh, and the abomination, and the mouse, shall be consumed together, saith the Lord.

And they shall go forth, and look upon the carcases of the men that have transgressed against me: for their worm shall not die, neither shall their fire be quenched; and they shall be an abhorring unto all flesh. For I know their works and their thoughts: it shall come, that I will gather all nations and tongues; and they shall come, and see my glory. And it shall come to pass, that from one new moon to another, and from one sabbath to another, shall all flesh come to worship before me, saith the Lord.

For as the new heavens and the new earth, which I will make, shall remain before me, you shall celebrate the feast of the LORD for seven days, with a rest on the FIRST DAY and a rest on the EIGHT DAY. You shall do the same with your oxen and with your sheep It shall be with its mother seven days; on the eighth day you shall give it to Me. And he carried me away in the spirit to a great and high mountain, and shewed me that great city, the holy Jerusalem, descending out of heaven from God, I saw no temple therein: for the Lord God Almighty and the Lamb are the temple of it. And the city had no need of the sun, neither of the moon, to shine in it: for the glory of God did lighten it, and the Lamb is the light thereof. And the nations of them which are saved shall walk in the light of it: and the kings of the earth do bring their glory and honour into it. And the gates of it shall not be shut at all by day: for there shall be no night there. And they shall bring the glory and honour of the nations into it. And there shall in no wise enter into it any thing that defileth, neither whatsoever worketh abomination, or maketh a lie: but they which are written in the Lamb's book of life.

When they have completed the days, it shall be that on the eighth day and onward, the priests shall offer your burnt offerings on the altar, and your peace offerings; and I will accept you, declares the Lord GOD. He that is unjust, let him be unjust still: and he which is filthy, let him be filthy still: and he that is righteous, let him be righteous still: and he that is holy, let him be holy still. And, behold, I come quickly; and my reward is with me, to give every man according as his work shall be. I am Alpha and Omega, the beginning and the end, the first and the last.

Then shall he say also unto them on the left hand, Depart from me, ye cursed, into everlasting fire, prepared for the devil and his angels. For I know their works and their thoughts: it shall come, that I will gather all nations and tongues; and they shall come, and see my glory. Blessed are they that do his commandments, that they may have right to the tree of life, and may enter in through the gates into the city. For without are dogs, and sorcerers, and whoremongers, and murderers, and idolaters, and whosoever loveth and maketh a lie.

See you there. Bring your works.
-Hashatan

Printed in the United States
by Baker & Taylor Publisher Services